Iron Butterfly

Iron Butterfly

A Novel of Africa

Clara Whaley Perkins

To order additional copies of this book, contact:
Xlibris Corporation
1-888-795-4274
www.Xlibris.com
Orders@Xlibris.com
101578

Dedicated to my father, Johnny C. Whaley, who migrated from South Carolina to Philadelphia with my mother and devoted his life to taking care of his family.

ACKNOWLEDGMENTS

I am grateful to my family for always cheering me on to complete my work. My deepest thanks to Reverend Dr. Leon H. Sullivan and to his organizations, whose work on the continent of Africa created opportunities for African Americans like me and Africans to recover the bond that made this story possible. I thank my editor, Angela P. Dodson for encouraging me to look deeper into my characters and story and for advising me well. Special thanks to Linda Wright Moore who always believed in my project and introduced me to Marie Brown, who helped me give the story focus; James Rahn for teaching me how to write fiction; and Renee Lucas Wayne for helping me develop the ability to craft a book. Finally, I thank my husband, Ralph Perkins, for his support, inspiration, and knowledge of Africa.

The North American Monark Butterfly migrates to the south,
flying over two thousand miles, year after year.
They survive storms and predators and return home in the spring.

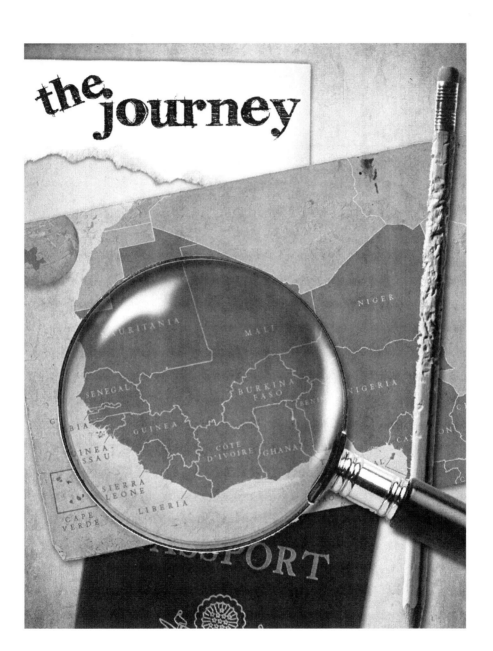

PROLOGUE

April 12

While Madame Chief sleeps, Catherine rises and takes down the blue velvet box that sits year-round on a shelf in the back of a closet in her bedroom. Inside is a small silver vial. She polishes it, fills it with the water that Madame Chief brought with her from a lagoon on the border between Sierra Leone and Liberia, and slips it into the breast pocket of her denim jacket. In another pocket, she places the packet of wildflower seeds. She awakens Madame Chief, and together they drive out to the farm, to the virgin earth that her father bought in New Hope, Pennsylvania, years before she was born. It takes an hour to get there. The farm is little more than a large field of tall grass. It sits back from the road. There is an old barn still standing, trees in the back acres, and a path that leads through the woods. The early-spring ground is wet, soft, and soggy. It gives underfoot, and the soles of Catherine's boots and Madame Chief's shoes are caked with mud by the time they reach the small clearing where the gravestone has been placed. Catherine had the stone put there in memory of her friends who died in the coup. Some of their precious belongings are buried there. The gravesite is covered with leaves and branches that had fallen during the winter. Catherine clears them away while Madame Chief sits on an old tree stump, silently reading the New Testament. From time to time, Madame Chief stops to sing a spiritual while Catherine labors. By the time she finishes the third or fourth song, Catherine's jacket hangs from the limb of a tree, and the tail of her shirt has been pulled free of her jeans. When the ground is laid bare, the forest seems to become still just as Catherine kneels on the rich, dark soil and takes the silver bottle from her pocket. She pours the water onto the earth while Madame Chief makes an impassioned plea to the ancestors to accept Catherine's offering. When the vial is empty, Catherine sits on the ground, closes her eyes, and feels the breeze. She remembers each of her friends—Bennet, Joy, Olivia, Luis—one at a time, then takes out the packet of wildflower seeds and casts the seeds over the grave.

CHAPTER ONE

March 31, 1992
Philadelphia, Pennsylvania

Pouring rain fell as Catherine eased her olive green BMW into a parking spot. The mail carrier was inside the foyer of her apartment house, sorting mail. *Perfect timing,* she thought.

Mama's letter should come today. It has to.

It was Friday. Madame Chief's letters often arrived at the end of the week.

There was an understanding between Catherine and Madame Chief, the female paramount chief Catherine met when she was a child living with her father, Marcus, in Sierra Leone. It had been honored since the day Catherine was forced to leave Africa, the day after the first coup d'état in Liberia's history, April 12, 1980. Madame Chief came to see Catherine in America. She arrived several days before the anniversary of the coup to help Catherine get through the residuals of the trauma it had caused her.

In spite of an unusual lapse in communication between them—the last letter had been delivered in February, over a month earlier—Catherine was certain that Mama, as she called her, would come. It was never a matter of *if* but when. With this confidence, she leaned back against the headrest and waited.

Waiting patiently was not something Catherine did well. Nevertheless, she was grateful for the unexpected moment of peace. It was the first time in weeks that she had come close to being able to sit still. If only for a moment her fears about the constant, shifting sands that were beginning to form the texture of her life were suspended. *Patience is good for some things,* she mused.

Her deep-set dark brown eyes fixed on the water cascading down the windshield as she listened to Stevie Wonder singing "Living for the City." It helped a little.

The chill that had met her as she came out of the apartment earlier that morning was gone.

It had been replaced by a stream of warm air making its way north, from as far away as the Gulf of Mexico. She welcomed it. Humidity filled the car and clouded the windows. It had puffed her shoulder-length curly dark hair into an Afro that delicately framed her high cheekbones and luminous, light, copper brown skin. She wore a white silk blouse, navy blue tailored suit, a London Fog raincoat, and of course, heels—typical dress for the child of a diplomat. The raincoat was usually in the trunk. She kept it there out of a habit formed through many rainy seasons in West Africa, where the skies had exploded with water one time too many.

The song ended. Catherine glanced up at the mail carrier to see if he had finished. *What's taking so long?* she thought. Her fingers fiddled with the silver locket hanging around her neck. It held a picture of Madame Chief. *I should have stayed on top of this,* she chided herself.

A new man in her life and end-of-semester calamities had distracted her, thrown her off guard, and kept her caught up in emotional mayhem for weeks. It was only after things had settled down that she realized that she hadn't heard from Madame Chief. The oversight had unsettled her. Impulsively, she had written to Madame Chief and had asked her point-blank about her plans for April 12. The inquiry felt rude and improper. Catherine had ended the letter with an apology for being so direct.

Finally, the mail carrier came out. Catherine buttoned the top button of her coat and reached for her umbrella, rain hat, and the snakeskin attaché case she carried to work. She opened the car door, and a man in a black trench coat appeared out of nowhere.

"Excuse me," he said, clutching the collar of his coat and sidestepping the door. His right hand clamped down on top of his black hat to keep it from blowing off. It was a Stetson. The kind men wore in the 1950s. His skin was ghostly pale. "Some storm!" he shouted over the roar of the wind, smiled, and hurried off. The recent stream of rainy days reminded her of the West African monsoon and how it ensured life. Life felt right when people smiled while walking in the rain.

Catherine recognized the man. He took care of the grounds around the convent for cloistered nuns directly across the street from the apartment building. She considered herself a Christian, but after the coup, she had lost the passion she had felt for Jesus since she was a child. But when she'd left her apartment this morning, her eyes fixed on the statue of Jesus standing in the nun's garden, and something stirred in her soul.

Catherine glanced over at the statue again as she got out of the car. *Perhaps I should look for a church,* she thought.

She walked toward the apartment building. Her slim torso swayed gracefully, unaffected by the sting of raindrops bouncing off concrete and nipping at her legs. She moved in the same manner as the young women of Sierra Leone. Of all the places she had lived, Sierra Leone was closest to her heart. Like an African market woman, she walked purposefully but did not hurry. Africans know that the faster you move in the rain, the more you get wet, and she was thoroughly Africanized. A strong wind came along and turned her umbrella inside out. She tried to close it, but the spokes broke at the joint, rendering it useless. The rain beat down on her shoulders and soaked through her raincoat and hat. The umbrella hung limply in her hand. Still, she refused to hurry. When she came to a trash can, she tossed it inside.

Her apartment was in the ideal location for Catherine. It was three blocks from Fairmount Park, where she ran for exercise. It was fifteen minutes from the Philadelphia International Airport and eight minutes from Amtrak's Thirtieth Street Station and quick trips to Washington, DC, and New York City. It was convenient to Philadelphia's best restaurants, theaters, hotels and museums, and the university where she taught art history and served as the curator for the university's collection of West African art.

Catherine was the only child of Marcus Lloyd, an American ambassador. Her mother, Susan, had died in a car accident in Rome when Catherine was five years old. After her mother's death, at her father's request, his mother Emma, a widower, came to Italy and raised Catherine until she was eight years old. When Nana Emma developed health problems, she went back to her home in Virginia to be close to her doctors, her other children, and her church—in that order—because she was a practical woman. Although it bothered her deeply to know that nannies would have to take care of Catherine, she was certain that her son would be thorough in his efforts to replace her, and he was. Marcus interviewed ten well-credentialed women before he finally settled on one. By nature, Catherine was fiercely independent, willful, and quick to take a position. More often than not, it was an unpopular one as far as the adults around her were concerned. So for several weeks after the nanny was hired, Marcus watched to see how Catherine got along with her and how the nanny handled Catherine. Each time he was reassigned to a new post, he went through the process again. It took time for each new nanny to win Catherine over. However, it was not a daunting task because Catherine was easy to get along with when she cared to be. In the end, she grew attached to each of them, though it did not happen easily because her grandmother had spoiled her and had left an indelible imprint against which they were measured. For her part, Nana Emma hoped she had also passed to Catherine the gift of discernment.

The American Embassy in Rome was her father's first post as an ambassador. He took her with him to all his posts: Switzerland, Laos, Paraguay, Sierra Leone, and Liberia. By the time Catherine returned to the States, she was almost eighteen years old, and she had lived most of her life in American compounds and had been educated in international schools. Catherine was as comfortable speaking other languages as she was speaking English.

Catherine stepped into the foyer and quickly inserted the key in the lock of the mailbox. Her name, Catherine Octavia Lloyd, was neatly typed on a sliver of white paper in a slot on the door. There were five white envelopes of varying sizes inside the box. She quickly went through them, looking for Mama's elegant penmanship. The letter was not there.

"*Merde,*" she cursed in French and slammed the mailbox shut. *This will not do,* she thought and started up the stairs. She checked her watch and calculated the time difference between Philadelphia and Freetown, Sierra Leone. *I'll call the embassy when I get upstairs and ask someone to go upcountry to Mokebe and find out . . . what?* Tension gathered between her shoulder blades.

The apartment was cool. The heat had been left off deliberately. Catherine hung up her coat and plopped down in a chair set close to an impressive collection of record albums, tapes, and CDs by Letta Mbulu, Fela Kuti, Hugh Masekela, Marvin Gaye, Miles Davis, Nina Simone, Gladys Knight and the Pips, Stevie Wonder, the Temptations, and others. Off came the heels. She put on headphones and closed her eyes and concentrated on the soulful voice of Nina Simone.

Her apartment had a view of the Philadelphia Museum of Art and the city's skyline. It was large, well-appointed, and welcoming. High ceilings, hardwood floors, a deck, and bilevel interior provided the sense of space that Catherine needed for psychological well-being. Smaller units made her claustrophobic. African carvings of wood and black stone on pedestals, shelves, and in corners appeased her taste for African artifacts. Handloomed rugs that had been purchased in bulk through a contact with rug makers in Cairo covered the floors and gave her bare feet pleasure. They were in every room, including the kitchen and bathroom. The apartment had a marble fireplace and built-in bookcases filled with rare books and African American literature. Sitting on the gleaming mahogany coffee table were two large books of beautifully photographed excursions into the land and cultures of Africa. Her housekeeper Queenie, a Jamaican woman with wide hips, a thick accent, and a no-nonsense attitude, had cleaned the apartment while she was out. Everything had been dusted and polished. Neatness and orderliness had been left in the Jamaican woman's wake. Queenie understood Catherine's habits. Catherine appreciated that. The slides she was organizing for her student's final exam had not been touched, even though Catherine had left them scattered on the coffee table.

When the tension had vanished from her back, Catherine took off the headphones. She went to the sofa and sat, picking up the slides. She stacked them in a box and thought about which of her friends in Sierra Leone she could ask to take a message to Madame Chief. It took a day over rough roads that often broke car axles to drive to Mokebe, the village where Madame Chief lived. It had to be someone who had a good car and could drop everything on notice. Everyone she knew working at the embassy had a late-model sedan, but of late they were tied up in embassy matters. Catherine sighed.

Lying under the slides was an invitation to a reception for Ambassador Aubrey Daniels, the newly appointed US ambassador to Liberia. The affair was being held in New York that very evening.

What's that doing there? She frowned. She hated Aubrey Daniels. She held him responsible for the death of the family members of her friends.

Aubrey had been her father's deputy mission chief at the time of the coup, his second in command. Marcus had gone to the States and left Aubrey in charge. Aubrey had refused to give asylum to the Americo-Liberians, who made it to the door thinking that America would protect them. Their ancestors were American slaves who had returned to Africa and set up a government that had strong ties to America. They were murdered in the streets outside the embassy.

Catherine picked up the invitation and went into the kitchen and dropped it in a trash can.

Suddenly she remembered that Jules Coleman, the deputy mission chief for the US Embassy in Sierra Leone, was in New York. Jules was like a brother to Catherine. He had mentioned that he was going to the reception. *Perhaps he knows what's going on with Mama,* Catherine thought. USAID, NGO representatives—nongovernment organizations workers—and other international types were going to be at the reception too. They were good sources of information, especially the rumors circulating the streets of Freetown. *Maybe I should go and put out feelers,* she mused. She reached inside the trash can and retrieved the invitation. *I suppose I could stomach Aubrey this one time,* she tried to convince herself. She tapped the invitation on her hand and stared at the pale notes penciled in on the calendar, the "things to do with Mama" list that should have been changed to ink marking definite plans by now.

The answering machine was blinking. There was one message. Catherine pushed the Play button, and a pleasant, cheerful voice with a hint of Southern accent sang out, "Hey, Cat. I got here earlier than planned." It was Justine, her best friend.

The sound of a small child's complaining voice was in the background. She pictured Justine's perennial smile, her head cocked to one side with the phone between her cheek and shoulder, and Sonya, the youngest of her three daughters, on her hip.

"Call me at my mom's when you come in. I've decided to stay until the end of the week. Mom and Dad are taking the kids shopping, so I'm free the rest of the day. See ya soon."

Catherine and Justine de Baptiste had met during their first year at Georgetown University. They shared a room in the dormitory. There was something about the peculiar complexity of their personalities that made them instantly comfortable with each other. On the surface, Catherine was cool and aloof. Justine was charismatic and charming, but she was much harder to get close to than most people guessed. During their senior year, they moved into an apartment off campus. Justine paid for her share of the rent with money she earned from modeling jobs. A pencil-thin, fair-skinned black woman with a smattering of light brown freckles on her narrow nose, Justine was extremely photogenic.

Justine was with Catherine on the first anniversary of the coup. She saw the dark place Catherine went into, how she stayed in the dorm filling page after page of her journal, how she dropped weight. Justine never forgot it. Every spring thereafter, when she noticed a change in Catherine's mood, she called Catherine two and three times daily until Madame Chief arrived.

Catherine dialed Justine's number.

"Hey, girl," Justine said. "How are you?"

"So-so," Catherine said in her mild British accent.

"Are you finished for the day? Do you want to hang out?"

Catherine looked down at the invitation. "How far can you go?"

"What do you have in mind?" Justine asked conspiratorially.

"I'd like to go to a reception in New York," Catherine revealed.

"New York!" Justine said excitedly. "I'm up for that. What time should I pick you up?"

"Make it an hour," Catherine suggested. "By the way, which one of your dad's cars are you driving?"

Justine liked fast cars. "The Jaguar."

Catherine hung up then went upstairs to her bedroom and straight to the shortwave radio. It was almost time for the African news.

On her bureau were several photographs: a picture of her mother and father holding hands on the steps of a cathedral in Venice; a picture of Madame Chief, seated and holding a staff; a holiday photo of her mother's brother, Nat, with his wife and children; and a black-and-white photo of Justine, Harold, and the girls. That left just enough space for a jewelry box and the radio. The radio was tuned to the BBC.

When she turned on the radio, a program showcasing an African American opera star appearing at the London Metropolitan Opera House was winding down. While Catherine changed into a black cocktail dress and heels, she pictured the massive stage of the theater and the singer standing on it. The opera ended on a dramatic note and a shower of applause. At the top of the hour, the familiar jaunty tune signaling the African news program began to play.

"There has been a resurgence of fighting among rebel forces positioned near the border between Liberia and Sierra Leone," the news reporter said.

Catherine walked over to the radio and stood next to it with her head down, her ear tuned to every word. "Refugees are fleeing this latest conflict. While new camps are being set up in Guinea and the Ivory Coast, food supplies have become a concern to aid workers who reported that raids on food distribution sites are depleting stores of rice and other staples. A member of the Catholic Relief Services reported . . ."

Fear formed in the pit of Catherine's stomach as reality set in. She was certain Mama was somehow involved with the situation unfolding at the border. She hoped that today was not a day she had planned to visit the refugee camps on the Sierra Leone side.

Dear God, if Mama's there, please watch over her. Provide her with safe passage. Give her the strength she needs to care for her people.

Catherine had not been to Sierra Leone in over a year, but her father and her friends working at the embassy had kept her apprised of the civil war in Liberia, which was spilling over the border into Sierra Leone. There was widespread concern that it would spread to other West African countries as well. Sierra Leone was on the verge of a crisis, and Madame Chief was right in the middle of it.

This is probably the reason I haven't heard from Mama. Maybe she is waiting to see if the situation will stabilize before she makes plans to leave but . . .

Dread came over her.

What am I going to do if Mama doesn't come this year?

Catherine was aware that the Economic Community of West African States (ECOWAS) had pushed the crises to the top of the G-8 agenda, making sure West Africa was not ignored. She watched PBS every night and listened to NPR to see how the most respected and influential arms of the press were covering the situation, knowing that every report put pressure on G-8. She was certain that America, England, France, Japan, Italy, Germany, Canada, and Russia—the members of G-8—had come to understand that something had to be done to stop the crises from affecting all West Africa. Sometimes she worried that their recent efforts had come too late. Aid to the beleaguered countries impacted by the civil war in Liberia had been stepped up. But the number of displaced people and the proliferation of rebel groups and warmongers had continued to grow at an alarming rate.

If it came down to a choice between leaving Sierra Leone in crises and coming to America to be with me for the anniversary, Mama would choose to be where she was needed most, in Sierra Leone.

The fear grew larger.

Catherine turned off the radio. She sat on the edge of her bed and stared out the window at the overcast sky. She remembered how she and Madame Chief would sit and watch soap operas when she came to America because Madame Chief was fascinated with them. It seemed like a strange thing to think about that at the moment.

What is this thing between Mama and me?

She went back to the living room, in search of the pillow Nana Emma had made for her before she died. It was at the bottom of the stack on the sofa. She pulled it out and wrapped her arms around it.

What is this thing between Mama and me? The thought repeated in her head. Her arms circled the pillow tighter.

Close to the first anniversary, she remembered waking up on a warm day in April, after a bitter winter. Marcus was out of the country. She went to his apartment and closed the shades in every room and just sat in the darkness. Hours later, when her friends figured out where she was, they had called her. She did not return their calls. When they caught up with her in class, Catherine made excuses for not calling them back. After class, she went back to her father's apartment and took the phone off the hook. This was not like her, not at all like her.

The sixteen-page letter that she wrote to Madame Chief during that time was filled with sad poems and bittersweet memories of her friends. The memories of that day were awakening. Springtime was a time of rebirth and renewal, but for Catherine, the season was inexorably twisted and tangled in the fragmented repressed memories of her friends' brutal slayings. Madame Chief had immediately responded to Catherine's letter and said she was coming to see her.

Still clutching the pillow, Catherine went to the window and peered down at the street below.

Mama, how am I ever going to do this without you?

A man came down the street and stopped in front of the statue of Jesus. His tan raincoat, soaked through, hung on his body like a wet dishrag. The man made the sign of the cross several times in rapid succession and climbed the stairs to the brick path leading to the chapel. This was only the second time Catherine had seen anyone go to the door of the chapel and ring the bell. She strained to see who was letting him in. The person stayed in the shadows, invisible to everyone except for the man standing at the door. He removed his hat and deferentially scraped the sole of his shoes on the steps before going inside. Catherine looked upward.

Is there something I'm supposed to learn from this?

She went back to the sofa and sat down.

Maybe I should ask my father or Justine to go to the gravesite with me this year.

Catherine ran her hands over the material of the pillow, smoothing it. She tried to imagine her father sitting on the tree stump, reading passages from the Bible, and could not quite picture it. It was easier to picture Justine on the stump, until she tried to imagine her singing tribal songs. The image was absurd no matter how Catherine turned it around in her head. And there were other problems, like the nuances that passed between Catherine and Madame Chief as they left her apartment, which could not be captured and put into words. She always walked behind Madame Chief, in a processional, from the door of the apartment, down the stairs, and to the car. It was the natural order. It was African. Catherine's heart sank. She bit her bottom lip.

What am I going to do?

She regretted that she had never invited her father and Justine to participate in the ritual.

It would have been easy enough. I did not intentionally leave them out. Or did I? Who's going to help me this year? I don't know how to do it alone. Why didn't I ever think about this before?

Her stomach tightened.

She tried to concentrate on what she had told her father and Justine about the ritual itself and came up blank.

Why did I decide to keep the ritual a secret?

She could not remember. The thought of describing it to either of them, now, made her shut down.

What is this thing between Mama and me? Why was it always just Mama and me?

Something in the question took hold of her. The clamor in her head subsided as her mind traveled back unimpeded over all the anniversaries, like pictures stored in a photo album. Carefully, she waded through them until she came to an image that explained why it had always been "just Mama and me."

Beyond the way to a garden of evergreens, where her friends waited to embrace her, something sacred had been spun between them.

Just Mama and me.

The phrase echoed in Catherine's head, and a particular year when they were at the gravesite came to mind. She had felt something then that she had not quite comprehended, but now the reason why it was always as it was became unmistakably clear.

Just Mama and me.

Time slowed down. Catherine sat straight up. In her mind's eye, she saw something just as she poured the sanctified water into the ground. She saw the essence of their souls, her own, and Madame Chief's, reaching out from their bodies and touching. It was amazing and utterly incredible. She felt like a child newly emerged from her mother's womb but still connected by an umbilical cord, a cord that had spanned the Atlantic Ocean.

The doorbell rang. She ignored it.

Just one more minute . . .

The rapture of the revelation spread through her.

It rang again. Reluctantly, she stood up and went to the intercom.

"Hello," she said and hoped that it was Justine and not one of her other friends stopping by on a spur of the moment. She did not have the wherewithal to entertain or be charming. Her emotions were all tied up in the revelation.

"It's me," Justine said. Her voice gently invited Catherine to return to reality.

"I'll be down in a minute."

"Take your time," Justine said. "I'll wait for you in the car."

Catherine grabbed a shawl and a purse from the hall closet. She quickly stuffed her wallet, lipstick, the invitation, and keys inside. As she opened the door, she glanced at the pillow on the floor. The urge to pick it up and go back to the sofa tugged at her. It pursued her as she hurried out the door and down the stairs.

CHAPTER TWO

March 31, 7:00 p.m.
Washington, DC

Marcus cleared the papers bearing the seal of the president of the United States off his desk. He stacked them in his briefcase. There was one folder that had been put to the side. He picked it up, opened it, and leafed through its contents. His heavy salt-and-pepper eyebrows knitted as he read the report for the third time since arriving in his office at 6:00 a.m. He was displeased. Frowning, he set the folder in his briefcase and closed it. He took off his reading glasses and wearily rubbed the bridge of his nose. His high-back chair creaked as he leaned back, clasped his thick-knuckled fingers behind his head, and contemplated the problems that had cropped up that day. The chair went backward as far as it would go as it cradled his six-feet-three-inch frame. Problems analyzed, he sat up and cracked his knuckles. The chair snapped back in place as he stood and reached for his dark gray suit jacket hanging on the shiny brass coatrack behind his massive desk. He put the jacket on over suspenders and silk tie. Marcus's shoulders were beginning to round but were still considerably square for a man his age.

The pictures on the walls of his office reflected his thirty-five years as a career ambassador. They spanned four changes in administration in the

White House, one photo each of him with the new president, his close-cut hair turning from black to distinguished gray. He was the diplomat they wanted and needed in West Africa.

Marcus was the quintessential diplomat. His career in the State Department was impressive; his credentials were stellar. He had been appointed the US ambassador-at-large for West Africa after the coup in Liberia. In effect, he was the United States' top administrator for the American embassies in the region, the only black man holding that position in the department. He oversaw the United States' involvement in West Africa while political and economic interest in West African governments had become considerable over the years.

Ready to wrap up business for the day, Marcus buzzed his secretary, Mrs. Jones.

"Mrs. Jones, would you please ask Jeremy to come to my office?" Marcus's baritone voice resonated.

"Of course, Ambassador."

Jeremy Hunter was Marcus's administrative aide. His modest dark suit hung on his thin, lanky frame like a clothes rack. He had an olive complexion, curly black hair, and alert turquoise eyes.

"Yes, Ambassador Lloyd," Jeremy said when he came in the office. He looked up at Marcus and ran his hand down the front of his tie. He was nervous.

Marcus looked at Jeremy over his reading glasses. "Did I get any calls?"

Jeremy reached inside his jacket. With one crisp movement, he pulled a notepad out of an inside pocket and flipped it open.

"Ambassador Chambers called from Ghana, Ambassador Taylor called from Senegal, and President Obasanjo returned your call," Jeremy said, reading from his notepad. Marcus was sorry that he had missed the call from President Obasanjo, the powerful leader of Nigeria.

"Your daughter called at four. She said she would call back later. And Jules Coleman called again."

"Before you leave tonight, call Jules's secretary and find out where he's staying in New York. It's the middle of the night in Sierra Leone, but I don't think she will mind. What's that, the fifth time he called?"

"I believe so, Ambassador."

Marcus reached for his jacket. He took off his glasses and carefully tucked them into the breast pocket and picked up his briefcase.

"I'm going to Philadelphia tomorrow to spend the day with Catherine. You can reach me at her apartment if you need anything. Confirm dinner with Ambassador Andrew Young. I told him I would get back to him today. Give him what he needs."

Jeremy nodded and wrote everything down with his usual efficiency.

"Is there anything else you want me to do before I leave tonight, Ambassador?"

"No. I think that's it. Thank you, Jeremy."

Jeremy left the room, reading over the notes and making new ones.

It was Friday night, but Marcus's aides and clerical staff were still in their offices, working on documents he needed to take with him to Nigeria. It was a rush job. Everything had to be ready by Monday. "Good night, Ambassador Lloyd," they each said as he passed the open doors to the offices strung along the corridor. He nodded and waved good-bye.

At the end of the hall, the elevator door was open. Marcus got on and pushed the button for the lobby. The elevator reached the ground floor and opened to the empty well-lit lobby of the State Department. "Good night, Ambassador," the security guards said as he passed their stations. His driver, a light-skinned African American man with a neat mustache, dressed in a dark suit, white shirt, and black tie, was standing on the curb smoking a cigarette. When he saw Marcus, he snuffed out the cigarette and stepped to the sedan.

"Good evening, Ambassador," he said and opened the door. His manner was formal but cordial.

"Good evening, Mr. Price," Marcus said. He gave Price the briefcase and climbed into the rear seat of the car. Price waited for Marcus to settle before handing him the briefcase and closing the door.

As a practice, Marcus addressed his staff over the age of thirty by their surname.

"Where to this evening, Ambassador?" Price said as he got behind the wheel.

"My apartment, please," Marcus replied.

A misty rain had begun to fall. Price turned the windshield wipers on and eased the dark blue sedan out onto the street.

"What time should I pick you up in the morning?" Price said over his shoulder.

"Nine o'clock. I'd like to catch the ten o'clock train to Philadelphia. Can you get a ticket for me tonight?"

"No problem, Ambassador."

"Thank you . . . How's that son of yours? The one in the air force."

"Doing real good, Ambassador Lloyd."

"Making a career in the service?"

"I believe so, Ambassador."

"Tell him to stop by my office the next time he's in town. I'd like to talk to him about his plans."

Marcus looked out the window, and a thousand thoughts about the American Embassy in Nigeria passed through his mind. The house that the US government had been ready to buy from President Obasanjo had not passed inspection—too many security issues. Another deal had to be negotiated, and quickly. The other countries with embassies in Nigeria were waiting to see if America would go along with the plan to move from Lagos to Abuja—no one wanted to do it. The new location, Abuja, was closer to where Muslims and Christians fought constantly. The problems were endless, and new ones cropped up daily.

"Mr. Price."

"Yes, Ambassador?"

"How many hours do you sleep at night?"

"What's that, Ambassador Lloyd?" Price looked at Marcus through the rearview mirror.

"I know it's a strange question."

"Not so strange, Ambassador . . . I'd say I get about six or seven."

"Do you ever have nights when you can't sleep?"

"Once in a while, not often, just when I'm stuck on something and can't shut my mind off."

Marcus could not remember the last time he slept five straight hours, or even four.

The car phone rang.

Marcus picked it up.

"Hi, Dad."

"Hi, Catherine. How was your day?"

Marcus was grateful to hear from Catherine. She had saved him the trouble of having to track her down.

"Not exactly what I was hoping for," Catherine said, "but I'm sure it will all work out. How was your day?"

"Tolerable. Jeremy said you called earlier."

"I did. I was just checking in. I'm in New York. Justine and I drove up this afternoon."

"What are you doing in New York?"

"Hanging out with friends."

Marcus's eyebrows shot up. Catherine was being evasive. She normally provided unsolicited details, names and places. It was her way of giving Marcus permission to keep track of her. That she was going to the reception for Aubrey Daniels never crossed his mind. The idea was too incredulous.

"Are you going back home tonight?"

"Well yes, I was planning to. Uh . . . why?"

"I thought we could spend Saturday together. I'm leaving for Nigeria on Tuesday."

Silence.

"Catherine, are you still there?"

"Yes, I'm here. What time are you coming to Philadelphia?"

"I should arrive around one o'clock. I'll call you when I get in."

"OK, Dad. Love you."

Marcus hung up the phone. He sensed that something was wrong. Whenever Catherine ended conversations with "love you," something was on her mind that she had decided to keep from him, usually because she thought it would burden him. It had started when they moved to Liberia, before she had become close with her friends. Although she hated it when he was called back to the States for meetings at the State Department or the UN, she never told him; instead she ended her calls to him with "love you." Many years later, she told him what she had felt during those times.

Marcus wondered if the something he sensed had anything to do with Madame Chief, but he dismissed it immediately. It was April. Madame Chief was coming. She would have called him if there had been a change in plans. He'd bet his life on it.

Traffic slowed to a crawl. Marcus looked over Mr. Price's shoulder. Ahead of them, cars snaked around a tow truck with a flashing red light.

Marcus sat back and wondered if Jeremy had reached Jules. That was another matter. *What was so urgent?*

"How are we doing, Mr. Price?"

"Not too bad. The back way to your apartment should be pretty clear," Price said as he reached the corner and took a right.

The phone rang.

"Ambassador Lloyd." It was Jeremy.

"Good evening, Jeremy. How's it going?"

"I just finished talking to Mr. Coleman. He was on his way out. He said he'll call you as soon as he comes back to his room in a half hour or so."

"Thank you, Jeremy," Marcus said and hung up.

Mr. Price pulled up in front of the building where Marcus rented a three-bedroom apartment. He parked and came around the car to open the door. It had stopped raining.

"Good night, Ambassador Lloyd. Have a good evening, sir," Price said as he closed the door behind Marcus. He tapped a salute on the rim of his hat with his index finger, got back in the car, and drove off.

Marcus shifted the briefcase from his right hand to his left and looked up at the sky. He seldom thought about Africa in a personal way. But the rain and the way Catherine had ended the conversation had triggered a memory.

The monsoon had been falling steadily for ten days. On the third day, the streets began to flood, and by the fourth day, there were endless pools of mud.

Their car got stuck in the mud a block away from the embassy. Catherine was still small enough to carry. Marcus picked her up, and she held on with one arm around his neck. Her nanny, an English woman named Mildred, followed close behind, walking in Marcus's footsteps. He gingerly stepped wherever the mud did not appear to be deep. Catherine leaned over to watch and laughed when Marcus underestimated how deep the water was. His foot sank low, and mud spilled into the cuffs of his pants. He held up one foot and then the other, shaking it and mumbling. "Is that your rain dance, Daddy?" she teased.

Marcus smiled briefly and looked upward at the moon and stars, and was reminded that he should never fail Catherine again as he felt he had the night of the coup in Liberia. From a thousand miles away, he had done everything humanly possible to provide for her rescue, but it had taken the American marines five hours to find her. She was locked up on the second floor in a room that faced the ocean. She had passed out on the floor. The bloody bodies of her friends were lying on the beach, clearly visible in the moonlight. He carried a burden of guilt that resurfaced every year as the anniversary approached. He sensed her pain.

The doorman opened the door to the lobby as Marcus approached the apartment building. Once inside the building, Marcus went straight to the elevator. On the way, he nodded to the people he recognized. Most of the tenants in the building were high-level government people from foreign countries on short-term assignments in Washington. Others were diplomats and businessmen who had taken yearly leases like Marcus in the pricey, upscale building.

Marcus's needs were modest. Although his apartment had as much square footage as a small house, it held just enough furniture. Every room was plainly furnished with the exception of the one that belonged to Catherine. His one indulgence was a custom-made leather recliner that sat opposite the television.

His stomach felt queasy. The conversation with Catherine had brought it on. Before settling into the recliner to watch tapes of March Madness, the NCAA basketball games, he poured the last of the milk in his refrigerator in a glass and drank it. It was barely enough to calm his stomach. He was glad the day was over.

The phone rang, exactly a half hour after the call from Jeremy.

"How are you, sir?" Jules Coleman said when Marcus answered the telephone.

Jules was a rising star in the corps of young American diplomats. Like Catherine, he grew up in American embassies. He had lived most of his life in Africa. Diplomacy was bred into him, and all things African was in his blood, except that he walked with a slight swagger like African American men. He was attracted to intrigue. When he wasn't "being the diplomat," he played sleuth, always interested in the direction of change in the world's governments. He was an information magnet.

"I'm fine, and how are you, Jules?" Marcus replied.

"Fine, sir."

"How is Celeste?" Marcus inquired. Celeste and Jules had been married less than a year.

"Well, sir, Celeste is pregnant."

Marcus felt Jules grinning through the telephone. "Congratulations, Jules," he said.

"Thank you, sir."

"Give Celeste my regards when you go home. And your parents, how are they?"

"Dad's had a cold that he's having a hard time shaking, but otherwise they're fine."

"The next time you talk to your dad, remind him that I'm going to be in Belgium in May."

"I won't have to, sir. He mentioned it when I called the other day. He's looking forward to seeing you."

"So what's going on? Jeremy told me you've been trying to catch up with me," Marcus said, curious about the reason for Jules's calls.

"It's about Madame Chief."

"What about Madame Chief?"

"She's missing."

CHAPTER THREE

April 1
Sierra Leone, West Africa

Madame Chief studied the four Liberian rebels from where she sat in the backseat of her car. It had been three days since they kidnapped her.

The rebel leader sat in the passenger seat. He was the oldest of the band, twenty-two years old. The others called him Aaron Sir. He was the only one dressed in army fatigues. The others wore T-shirts and shorts. Aaron wore gold-rimmed sunglasses that he never took off. He did this deliberately to intimidate his men. Madame Chief took an instant dislike to him. He had pointed a gun at her driver's head.

She was on her way to Freetown to deal with an urgent matter when the rebels commandeered her car. They had placed a tree across the road and waited in the bushes. When Benjamin was forced to stop, they jumped out and surrounded the car. Each one nervously wielded an AK-47. "Get out or I will blow your brains out," Aaron had said to Benjamin, Madame Chief's driver of thirty years. Benjamin had not moved. "Mama, what should I do?" he had said, turning to her. Madame Chief had rolled down the window and said to Aaron, "There is no need for that. We will not resist, but you must not threaten my driver. Is that clear?"

For Benjamin's sake, Madame Chief had allowed them to hold her captive.

Aaron never directly threatened Benjamin again, but he treated him poorly. Several times, he had taken him aside, out of earshot, spoken to him, slapped and kicked him. Madame Chief never found out what Aaron had said to Benjamin before beating him because Benjamin would not tell her.

The rebel driving Madame Chief's tan Mercedes sedan was named Mohamed. Mohamed was sixteen years old. He was a new recruit and had not been indoctrinated yet. He had been singled out to go with Aaron the day after he joined the rebels. When he was not behind the wheel, he sat with glasses on, reading one of the worn paperback novels that he carried in his backpack. He seemed to be more interested in reading his book than promoting their "mission," as they called her abduction. Joe, on the other hand, saw this as a chance to locate and fight enemy rebels living in the bush, which was also a part of the mission. He was also a new recruit and the youngest of the group, fourteen years old. Joe was restless and quickly bored. He seldom kept quiet and "always kept something going," Mohamed would say. Blaze, the only experienced member of the threesome, was a veteran child soldier. He was seventeen years old. He wore a woman's red wig and a bra over his T-shirt. His eyes were bloodshot, and he smelled of cannabis.

The car hit a hard bump, and everyone surged forward. Mohamed slowed down to navigate a series of potholes in the dirt road. The bush was overgrown, suggesting that no one had driven this way in some time. Madame Chief wondered if they knew where they were.

A miniature New Testament small enough to carry in her pocket was on her lap. When the car swerved again, it almost fell off. She steadied it with one hand and took out the last letter Catherine had written to her. As she held it against her chest, she remembered the last time she had seen Catherine and the last anniversary. She was not sure how long she drifted, but it seemed as though the light of the day was waning when she finally looked again around at the rebels.

Madame Chief had refused to speak directly to the rebels for two days. She would not allow them to do anything for her. All communication between them and her had gone through Benjamin. Now, she was ready to talk to them.

"Do you know who I am?" Madame Chief said in a quiet but authoritative tone. Her voice was deep. She articulated every word clearly and plainly. She spoke as if she was being generous in speaking to them.

Everyone in the car turned and looked at her, surprised.

"Yes, madame," Aaron said. "We know who you are."

She was the most famous woman in West Africa. Her picture was frequently published in West African newspapers. There was no other woman in West Africa with her influence. She was both a queen and a public figure.

Madame Chief was seventy-two years of age. Her face was full of character. There was calm spirituality in her noble carriage and in her eyes.

She was dressed in a lime green brocade dress, fashioned in layers that draped to the ground. Her head wrap was made of the same material as the dress. It sat high above her head like a crown. She wore gold leather sandals. There was no mistaking who she was.

"I wanted to make sure that you know what you were doing," Madame Chief said calmly, looking down the high bridge of her narrow nose.

Joe started making a clucking noise with his tongue.

"Stop that, Joe," Aaron snapped.

Joe slouched down in the seat and pulled his baseball cap down over his eyes. He peeped at Madame Chief.

"What rebel band do you belong to?" Madame Chief said to no one in particular.

Joe pushed his hat back and sat up. "We are members of the Liberian Revolutionary Front for Freedom and Democracy," he boasted and flashed an easy smile.

"Who?" Madame Chief exclaimed as if she has not heard of them when, in fact, she had.

"The LRFD," the boy repeated. "We are fighting against Charles Taylor."

"What are you doing in Sierra Leone? Charles Taylor is not here," Madame Chief said with annoyance.

The smile melted from Joe's face. Baffled, he looked around at the others. The message was lost on him but not on Aaron, who frowned in disgust. Mohamed looked at Madame Chief through the rearview mirror with interest. Blaze turned and watched the dense bush pass by the side window. His hand gripped the barrel of an AK-47.

"We have come to get recruits," Joe said.

"Do I or my driver look like candidates?" Madame Chief replied roughly.

Aaron shot Joe a warning look.

"You are wasting my time," Madame Chief said to Aaron. "What do you want with me? Tell me quickly."

"Stop the car!" Aaron barked. He got out, drew his pistol, and pointed it at Benjamin. "Get out of the car," he said, waving it at him.

"What are you doing? How dare you! Stop pointing that gun at my driver. Now!" Madame Chief demanded. The force of Madame Chief's command caused a knee-jerk obedience to her royal African bloodline, and Aaron was thrown off balance. His will to do whatever he had in mind to do to Benjamin shut down.

"This is the last time I am going to tell you to not point your gun at Benjamin. If it happens again, we will get out and I dare you to stop us."

Aaron looked at her blankly. He walked a little ways from the car, stopped—as if to clear his head—then got back in.

"Drive," he snapped at Mohamed.

Madame Chief was shaken. Her heart raced out of control as she settled back into the seat.

There was, however, no outward indication of this. She stared out the window and lightly fanned her face with Catherine's letter. Her mind reeled. She wanted to demand that Aaron take her to a village. But she was afraid of pushing him again. She looked at Benjamin. He was trembling. She called his name.

"Benjamin."

"Yes, Mama."

Madame Chief touched Benjamin on the shoulder.

"Do not be afraid," she said in Mende. Benjamin drew a deep breath, then relaxed.

Before deciding what to do next, Madame Chief needed more information about Aaron, his intentions, and if the mission was fact or fantasy.

Everyone was silent for several miles. Even Joe was quiet.

"Do you know how far you have come into Sierra Leone?" Madame Chief said to Aaron.

"Yes, madame. I have an idea," Aaron responded blandly.

His response irritated her.

"What could you possibly want with me, an old woman?" she asked.

"Do not worry, madame. No harm will come to you," Aaron said, looking out the window.

"What do you mean 'no harm will come to me,'" she snapped at him, unable and unwilling to restrain her irritation. "Are you a stupid man? If anything happens to me, my people will enter your country and kill you and your family and all your relatives. I do not think that you are so stupid as not to know that. I think you should be wise and avoid this chance you are taking. Doesn't your country have enough problems?"

"Madame, we will not keep you long. You will be home in a very short time," Aaron said coolly.

"Where are you taking me?" Madame Chief demanded. She leaned forward so that her words would fall directly on Aaron's ear.

"To Liberia," Aaron said.

"Where in Liberia?"

"Just across the border."

"Why there?"

Aaron turned, looked at the side window, and fell silent.

They emerged from the bush onto a road Madame Chief recognized. They were headed northwest. Several miles later, they turned off the road and headed back into the bush.

"Do you know where you are going?" Madame Chief asked Aaron.

No response.

Joe piped up, "Aaron Sir knows all the back roads in Sierra Leone," he said.

"I see," Madame Chief said. Her eyes narrowed.

"Why do you carry a gun?" she asked Aaron after a while.

"Because it is necessary," he said.

"Necessary for what?"

"For change."

"You and your men obviously have a plan," she said to Aaron. She was almost civil. It took him by surprise. He turned to look at her.

"I see that you are the one most committed to your cause," Madame Chief said to him. "The name of your army, what do you call it—the Liberian Revolutionary Front for Freedom and Democracy—rings hollow to my ear. I don't think any of you know the meaning of the word *revolution*."

Madame Chief turned to Joe. "You were probably just looking for something to do when the LRFD came through your village."

Joe pulled his cap up and said, "How did you know that?"

Madame Chief ignored him. She leaned forward, just far enough to study Blaze. He was checking his gun.

"You with the gun, Blaze. Is that your name?"

"Yes, madame," Blaze replied.

"How many people have you killed, Blaze?"

"Madame, you don't want to know that."

"Many?" she inquired.

"Yes, madame, many," Blaze said.

"How many men do you think you will have to kill for the problems in your country to be solved?" Madame Chief pressed.

Blaze looked at her puzzled.

"Answer me," Madame Chief insisted.

"I don't know," Blaze muttered and turned his head to look out the side window.

"Guess. Do you think a hundred? A thousand? Ten thousand? A million? How many?"

"I don't know, madame. As many as it takes," he said flatly.

"Let me tell you something, Blaze. You could kill all of the people you call the enemy of your country and not solve a single problem. Do you really think guns are the solution to your problems? Guns have never solved anything. Using peaceful means is the only way to solve the problems in Liberia."

Turning to Aaron, Madame Chief said, "I don't know what you have in your mind to do with me. I see that some crazy idea has hatched in your head, but whatever it is, be quick about it. I have important business in Freetown."

Madame Chief sat back, opened the small Bible, and began reading.

CHAPTER FOUR

April 1, 11:00 a.m.
Philadelphia, Pennsylvania

Marcus took an early train to Philadelphia and checked into the Four Seasons Hotel. He needed a place to think about the information Jules was bringing with him from New York before he saw Catherine.

He waited for him in the hotel's restaurant.

Jules walked into the restaurant like a man with a purpose. He spotted Marcus and made his way to the table.

His light skin was tanned, his clear alert eyes, dark hazel. He was not exactly handsome, but women found him attractive. Jules was thirty-four years old, four years older than Catherine.

Marcus stood up, and they shook hands the way a father and son might, genuinely glad to see one another without having to say so. Jules handed Marcus a file.

Before leaving Sierra Leone, Jules had asked his research assistant, John Caesar Palmer-Shaw—JC as they called him—to collect as much information as possible about the circumstances of Madame Chief's abduction and bring it to him in New York. JC was Madame Chief's grandson. He had twenty-four hours to pursue the task. Jules had met him at the airport when his plane landed.

The file contained an official report of Madame Chief's kidnapping and other information JC had pulled off the wire. Most of it was accounts of Liberian rebels crossing the border into Sierra Leone. JC filled Jules in on the rumors circulating the streets of Freetown, the mood of the country as the word began to spread, and anything else he thought would be helpful to Jules. He revealed his personal feelings and thoughts on the matter of his grandmother's abduction, things he had thought a great deal about but had not discussed with anyone until now. When they'd finished, JC had taken the first plane back to Africa.

The restaurant was posh. The tables were set with fine china and linen. The waiters were efficient. They brought menus, water, and bread then hovered nearby for requests. Everyone spoke in hushed tones.

Marcus was wearing a light blue knit shirt that Catherine had given him the previous Father's Day. He pushed up his sleeves and opened the file. The expression on his face never changed as he breezed through the contents. Jules watched him and occasionally looked around the room to see who had come in.

Finally, Marcus closed the file.

"Do you know about the problem between Madame Chief and Minister Fofana?" Jules asked, locking his fingers and leaning forward on the armrests.

"I've heard things," Marcus said. "How about filling me in?"

"Madame Chief is pushing a bill to keep better tabs on what's coming out of the diamond mines. Minister Fofana and his people have been nitpicking the wording of the bill, saying the taxes are too heavy and could hurt business. But there's a chance the bill will get through as is. You know how she feels. She's made it clear that the profits from the diamonds should be used to serve the people, not the government. Remember what she said about diamonds in her speech to the UN? How did she put it? 'People need food! Diamonds cannot be digested.'"

Marcus smiled.

"How hard is she pushing?" Marcus asked.

"Very hard."

"Minister Fofana is probably the most powerful minister in Sierra Leone. But have you heard that he and President Payne have a substantial stake in Sierra Rutile?"

"I've heard rumors," Marcus said. "Why?"

"I was having a drink at Steven's Bar a couple of months ago and got into a conversation with someone representing a South African mining company. He had put in a bid on a site but didn't get it and was grumbling about it. He got drunk and let it slip out that Foday Payne had led him to believe he would get the contract."

"What are you making out of that?"

"Since Foday Payne took control of the country, Sierra Rutile is beating out the other West African–based mining companies. The other companies winning bids on a regular basis are companies no one's heard of."

"So you think Fofana and Payne are working with them?"

"It looks like it. These fly-by-night companies are probably fronts, Marcus."

"I know. We've suspected for some time that the diamonds for the coups are being laundered through them."

"I've heard that the vice president of Sierra Rutile is one of Foday Payne's closest friends," Jules added. "The family is well connected in the global market. Most of the financial backing for the company comes from Europe and South Africa. Their bloodline goes back as far as Madame Chief's."

"Interesting," Marcus replied. "Foday is covering all the bases to make sure he gets his share of everything Sierra Leone has to sell. That man's a big problem for his country." Marcus frowned. "We're going to have to put more pressure on him to hold elections . . . get the UN, ECOWAS, and G-8 more involved."

"If something's not done quickly, Sierra Leone could be headed down the same path as Liberia," said Jules. "There are already signs. Foday's army is beginning to fracture, and to complicate things, De Beers is starting to pay top dollar for Sierra Leone's diamonds. Lately, no one is even trying to deny that there's a link between the diamonds being smuggled out of the mines and the guns that were bought to back Foday's coup. It's as if no one cares as long as they get their cut."

"What's the connection between the rebels who kidnapped Madame Chief and Minister Fofana?"

"I'm not sure there is one. It's just that Foday's name keeps popping up whenever anyone talks about it," Jules replied.

"Why?"

Jules shrugged. "Some sort of coincidence maybe."

"How's that?"

"Maybe people don't believe this much trouble could fall on Madame Chief. Personally, I think they're making a connection because about a month ago, Fofana really tried to do a number on Madame Chief. There's speculation that Sierra Rutile hired the people who tried to force Madame Chief to sign off on a letter giving them permission to survey her land, but we know that the entire business was handled through Minister Fofana's office."

"I'm not sure I understand this. What's his interest in a fishing village?"

"Our sources say that diamonds may have been found in her village."

"That's impossible!"

"Let me correct that. The diamonds are somewhere in No Way Out."

"Nobody goes there!"

"Well, somebody did."

"I guess if diamonds were going to be found anywhere in Mokebe, No Way Out would be the logical place," mused Marcus. "Have you ever been there?"

"No," said Jules. "Never cared to."

"I passed through a part of it once with a very experienced guide. Sunlight barely reaches the ground. It's a maze of trees, streams, and swamps, filled with all kinds of fever and lizards. No one voluntarily goes in."

"I've heard that some villagers have gotten lost in there and wandered for months," Jules said.

"There's a lot of folklore about No Way Out," Marcus responded. "Ask Catherine about it sometime. She wrote a paper about it when we lived in Sierra Leone, interviewed quite a few people. She told me that the villagers believed it's cursed and filled with evil spirits. They say that when someone gets lost, the good spirits come out to do battle with the bad spirits and show villagers the way out. People claim it plays tricks with your mind. After visiting it, I understand why. There's medicinal vegetation on the periphery. That's usually as far as people will go." Marcus paused. "I find it hard to believe that Fofana found out about the diamonds before Madame Chief did. People go out of their way to give her information. How big is the cache supposed to be?"

"I don't know. Information on that is sketchy."

"It has to be big enough for Minister Fofana to go through the trouble," Marcus reasoned.

"There's no doubt about that," Jules agreed. "But the way he's handled the situation has made him a very unpopular guy. On the other hand, everyone seems to be looking the other way. I think people are afraid of him. Do you remember the story about the paramount chief who was found in the trunk of a car after being missing for three days?"

"No, I didn't hear about that."

"It blew over fast. But some people think Minister Fofana was involved."

"How?"

"That's not clear."

"I see," said Marcus. "But Fofana's a smart man. I have to believe he's aware that behaving sadistically with Madame Chief is bound to hurt his interests in the long run. He can't afford to alienate locals if they're going to set up a dig in her district. Things are bad in Sierra Leone, but it wouldn't surprise me if the men in the village are passing on this one."

"Maybe."

"What do you mean?" Marcus asked.

"Jobs are more scarce than ever, Marcus. Have you seen the latest exchange rate? It was released a week ago. Sierra Leone's money is just about worthless now, and the infrastructure is falling apart. There's no real money to pay the workers. It's all in the report I sent you last week."

Marcus thought about the stack of reports he had not been able to get to and shifted in his chair. Jules was right. Military coups often preceded the problems like the ones Sierra Leone was having.

"I've gone a long way to get around to my point, which is that no one with authority seems to be in a hurry to find Madame Chief. Her bill comes up for a vote in a week. If she doesn't come home soon, it will be up to the other supporters to get it through. You and I know the opposition will kill it if she's not around. That's what makes the timing of her abduction interesting."

Marcus's eyebrows shot up. "How so?"

"It's probably nothing," said Jules, "but bad things often come in spades, especially in West Africa."

"Come on, Jules. What is it?"

Jules hesitated.

"Eyewitnesses said she was kidnapped by Liberian rebels."

"I read that part," Marcus said.

"JC told me that they said there was something strange about the rebels. They seemed to be carrying a lot of equipment, as if they had everything they needed for a long journey in their backpacks. They had more food than ammunition. What rebel travels like that? I have to wonder if they were Liberian rebels at all. You know what I mean?"

"I'm not sure I do."

"People *assumed* they were Liberian rebels."

"What are you suggesting, Jules?" Marcus said, thinking that maybe Jules was getting too caught up in the intrigue.

As if Jules had read his mind, he said, "Just hear me out, Marcus. It just strikes me as more than a coincidence given everything that's happened lately."

"And you think Fofana's involved?"

"Fofana doesn't mind using kidnapping to get what he wants."

"That's really risky. What if something goes wrong?"

"Then the finger will be pointed at the Liberian rebels."

"I see," Marcus said thoughtfully, beginning to think that Jules might be on to something. But at the moment, the trail was too muddled. There was too much speculation. He needed something more concrete for Catherine's sake.

"Anything else?" Marcus asked.

Jules cleared his throat. "There is one other thing."

"Well, what is it?"

"Madame Chief has a heart condition."

She's been keeping that from Catherine.

"What a mess," Marcus muttered under his breath, shaking his head. "Is that it?"

"That's all of it."

"Thanks, Jules. Let's touch base at the end of the week."

Marcus went to his room. He sat down in a chair facing the television and considered his options.

He could put off telling Catherine about Madame Chief for a couple of days and hope that the rebels came to their senses, or he could tell her everything when he saw her.

The problem with the first option was that she might run into someone who would tell her before he did. Catherine was well connected in the international community. She had more friends than Marcus had ever been able to keep track of. Transatlantic calls routinely ran up her phone bills. Collectively, her network was an information pipeline for rumors, speculations, innuendo, overheard conversation, and eyewitness accounts of incidents that took place in the most remote and unseemly places. Dread washed over Marcus when he thought about how Catherine would be affected when he told her about Madame Chief.

He recalled how Catherine and Madame Chief came to be close.

Catherine was ten years old when Marcus took up his post in Sierra Leone. After he presented his credentials to the president of Sierra Leone, Siaka Stevens, the embassy staff hosted a reception. Invited were high-level government officials, leaders of the business community, and the country's paramount chiefs. Madame Chief arrived early to introduce herself to Marcus and to Catherine because she had not planned to stay. Catherine stood next to Marcus on the receiving line, and everyone waited patiently while Madame Chief welcomed her to Sierra Leone. For reasons known only to Madame Chief, she decided to stay. During the reception, Marcus noticed Catherine approaching Madame Chief, who was sitting alone. Catherine sat down beside her, and they talked for the remainder of the night until the reception ended.

A month later, Madame Chief sent Marcus and Catherine an invitation to visit her in her village. Catherine had neglected to tell Marcus that she had asked Madame Chief if she could visit her there. Unbeknownst to Marcus, Catherine and Madame Chief had exchanged letters. This came to light when Madame Chief stopped by the embassy to see Catherine one day. It took a moment for Marcus to remember who she was when the marine passed her request to him. When Catherine was told that Madame Chief was there, she ran into the room. Marcus invited Madame

Chief to join them for lunch. Openly, Madame Chief shared her personal information, describing her beautiful village and how she had come to be the second female paramount chief to be elected to Sierra Leone's Parliament just days after she became a widow. She talked about her children and grandchildren, how their names were chosen in accordance with African tradition and where they lived in the world. She asked how Catherine liked the International School. She felt free to ask about Catherine's mother. Marcus told her about his career as a diplomat. Impressed that she was not asking for anything, that she was extending friendship to Catherine, he relaxed.

At the first opportunity, a tour of the villages in Madame Chief's chiefdom was scheduled. The day after they arrived, Catherine developed a fever. She stopped shivering whenever Madame Chief placed her hand on her forehead. When the fever broke, Madame Chief insisted that Marcus continue his plan. He visited villages during the day and, at the end of the day, returned to her village, Mokebe, to be with Catherine until she had fully recovered. Catherine's days with Madame Chief were spent walking along the beach, following Mama from place to place in the village, listening to stories about Sierra Leone. Madame Chief entertained Catherine with folktales about Bra Spider, Bra Babbu, and Bra Cunny Rabbit, which she later recounted to Marcus. Not long after this, Catherine began calling Madame Chief Mama, and Madame Chief referred to her as her spiritual daughter.

Marcus stood up and turned on the television to CNN. Then he called room service and ordered milk.

CHAPTER FIVE

April 1
Philadelphia, Pennsylvania

The first thought that came to Catherine when she awoke at 11:30 a.m. was, *Where is Mama?*

She turned on her side and looked out the window at the sky. The sun was shining. The sheer white curtains at her window fluttered with the morning breeze. A blue stained-glass butterfly suspended by a silver thread hung in front of the glass pane. The blue glass caught the sunlight and sparkled as the butterfly swung from side to side as if restless to take flight. When Madame Chief gave it to Catherine, she had said, "When I saw this, I thought of you, my dear. You seem content to live in the garden, but you constantly move from one flower to the next, never tiring, and you let nothing get in the way of the task. You are spirit-like . . . like this iron butterfly. Spirits are enduring. Always remember that."

Catherine closed her eyes and pictured Madame Chief in her garden, walking along the rows of cassava plants, inspecting the leaves, her plain cotton dress and wide-brim hat tied under her chin fluttering to the breeze drifting off the Atlantic Ocean. Warm biscuits and lavender was what Catherine thought Mama smelled like when she enveloped her in a hug.

Catherine opened her eyes and sat up to think about the reception from the night before. Nothing had worked out. Jules had avoided her, and the flimsy bit of information offered to her by the aides who had just come back from Sierra Leone in the past week made her wonder why she had bothered to make the trip. Sierra Leone's Parliament was scheduled to meet, and Madame Chief was expected to be there. That was all anyone had to say. Jules had come and mingled a little. "There's something I have to take care of. I'll call you tomorrow," he had said, backing away from her and making a quick exit when she began asking questions about Madame Chief.

Jules seemed awfully anxious to get away, Catherine mused. *Maybe I'm just being paranoid. He's always on the move,* she reminded herself. She rolled out of bed and slipped into sweats.

After retrieving Saturday's *Philadelphia Inquirer* from the front step, she hurried back up to her apartment and tossed it on the kitchen table next to Friday's *Inquirer*, which she had not yet read. She satisfied her curiosity about the local news by reading the *Inquirer* and the *Philadelphia Tribune*. The *New York Times* and the *Washington Post*, which she had already read the day before, sat in a heap on the chair. She read the *Times* and *Post* daily for the international news. Both papers usually carried one story about West Africa.

She prepared a pot of coffee for that necessary first cup of the day and decided to read Friday's *Inquirer* first.

The front page was dominated by a story about a child molester. Catherine glossed over it and browsed the following pages for news about Africa.

On page 26, a story headlined NAMIBIA TO KILL WILDLIFE TO FEED HUNGRY caught her eye. Midway through the second paragraph, she dismissed it as negative propaganda. On page 37, there was a story about a US representative who had visited Lincoln University, a small historically

Black university in rural Pennsylvania, and passionately petitioned the student body and faculty to support efforts to send aid to Africa. "African Americans will have to lobby and lobby hard for Africa if that continent is to receive the kind of US attention and aid given to other nations," the politician was quoted saying. She remembered with nostalgia the day she had gone with Marcus to visit Lincoln. He'd given a talk about US foreign policy in Africa. Afterward, they had toured the campus, and Marcus talked about friends from his hometown who had gone to Lincoln during the 1950s. The memory was less poignant than it would have been had she thought about it on any other day. It faded as she turned the page. She gulped coffee and restlessly scanned the pages, looking for something in the black ink to calm her. Eventually, she tossed the paper aside and picked up the Saturday *Inquirer.* She turned the pages, quickly leafing through the paper, looking for other news about Africa. She was disappointed. There was no news about Sierra Leone.

She had an urge to run.

An hour should do it, she thought, calculating the amount of time spent pounding concrete that it would take to get rid of the troublesome feelings building up inside her. She knew she'd run longer—and harder—if she had to in order to shake the unease out of her system.

She started out walking in the direction of Fairmount Park four blocks away. When she reached the Philadelphia Museum of Art, which anchored the front end of East and West River Drives, she picked up the pace—pumping her arms, beating the air, and thinking about the reception.

At the reception, she had avoided a confrontation with Ambassador Aubrey Daniels. Luckily, he hadn't been there when she arrived. Nor was he there when she left. But that was the only thing that had gone her way.

No one with information about Sierra Leone could—or would—tell her much more than she already knew. Those who knew more avoided the subject of Madame Chief. They asked her if she had spoken to Jules or

Marcus about it. However, one chatty aide to Ambassador Carrington, the son of a friend of President Bush, had gone on and on about how the war in Liberia "was spreading like a virus to Sierra Leone and how helpless the paramount chiefs were." He was new to the corps of diplomats and their gatherings, still becoming familiar with who sat in the biggest chairs in the house. He did not know who Catherine was. Finally, one of the other aides noticed the strained expression on her face. He took the aide aside and explained things to him.

On the way out, Catherine had run into Thomas Massaqua, an expatriate from Liberia. He recognized her before she recognized him. He had aged. The affection in his eyes and the sincerity in his voice helped her remember what he looked like before the coup.

He'd greeted her in the European custom of touching cheeks, first one, and then the other. He then told her that everyone in his family was dead except for him and one of his daughters. "I'm one of the lucky ones," he said. The rebels had looted his house, raped and stabbed his wife, shot him and his five children, and left them all for dead. A neighbor found him. "Praises be to Allah," he said after he'd told Catherine the story. He threw up his hands and pressed his palms together prayerfully. "He took us to the doctor. The soldiers also used the doctor," he explained breathlessly. "The soldiers were so drunk they were accidentally shooting one another."

Soldiers wounded by bullets from the same guns that were probably used to kill my friends.

The thought had made her angry. She ran harder.

Although his spirit was lighter when they parted, Catherine's was heavier. His burden had been transferred to her. "I'm ready to go now," she had said, turning to Justine as she pressed back tears of sadness for him and for herself.

Catherine ran until the sorrow that was weighing down her spirit was thrown off. She ran until the madness of the world became a whisper carried off by the wind. She ran until the misery tearing at her was tamed. Fearlessness grew with the beat of her pulse. As she ran, she grew stronger. She grew calmer. Purged, she stopped and walked home.

She passed under the shadow of the statue of Jesus, standing with his palms raised and poised in a promise of absolution and compassion. Catherine looked up at it. She felt better.

She bounded up the stairs to her apartment. She decided to take a shower and get dressed to be ready to pick up Marcus when he called. She had decided to talk to him about Madame Chief, to ask him for his help.

When she came out, she tied a towel around her waist, leaving her breasts bare like an African woman. She wrapped another one around her wet hair. She felt free and unburdened. *I'll be all right,* she mused, pleased that she felt some optimism even though the anniversary of the coup was approaching and nothing had been resolved. She rubbed her hair with the towel and thought about clearing the gravesite alone.

The phone rang.

"Hi, Catherine. How are you?"

The voice was deep, smooth, and intimate. It was the voice of a man who loved women.

Clifton Hayes was the new man in Catherine's life. He was a former baseball player turned businessman, with an MBA from Wharton. He was a very good-looking guy—just shy of six feet and athletically built. Clean shaven and well raised, Clifton was just about everything her single black girlfriends were looking for in a man. He was also one of Harold's friends. When Justine introduced him to Catherine, he looked at Catherine as if he had been waiting for her all his life.

Several weeks—and several dates—later, Justine told Catherine that he was married.

"I never met her. They were separated by the time he moved north," Justine had explained guiltily. "She's still living in Atlanta, I think. No kids.

She's a lot older than us. I think she's about thirty-five," Justine said, being catty. "He's thirty like us . . . Anyway, a friend of his told me it was over between them before it really got started. I was waiting to see if you liked him before I told you. Now don't bless me out, girl."

Catherine was not particularly surprised to learn that Clifton was married. Somehow she had picked up on it. Still, she wondered how long it was going to take him to tell her about his wife. She decided to give him until the end of the week to tell her. The clock was ticking on his character.

The next time they went out, Clifton told her that he was in the process of getting a divorce and that it would be final soon. Then he promptly went out of town on business, giving Catherine just enough time to think things over. When he came back, she told him—in a matter-of-fact, even-toned, nonnegotiable manner—"I've thought about your situation and decided that maybe we should not see each other for a while. I don't believe in getting involved with 'almost divorced' men." It was not what she wanted to do; it was what she *had* to do because Clifton had already become the last person she thought about before going to sleep. The next day, he'd sent her a bouquet of flowers with a card that simply said, "Please?"

"Clifton," said Catherine. "How are you?"

Catherine had not expected to hear from him so soon after breaking it off. Warmth spread through her body in an instant. She thought about his eyes, the way he caressed her with them. She found a chair. She had to sit down.

"Fine now," he said.

The masculine smoothness in his voice made her want to throw off her towel and pull him into her bed.

"How have you been?"

The question reminded her of what she had just come through. She was not sure what to tell him.

"So-so," she said. "How was your trip to LA?"

"Pretty good. The weather was fine," Clifton said casually.

"Business or pleasure?" Catherine inquired. She relaxed and cradled the phone gently between her ear and shoulder.

"I went out there to see a friend of mine."

Catherine's heart flipped. *A woman?* "Anyone I know?" she hedged. *What a stupid question. Get a hold of yourself.*

She wished it didn't matter who he had gone to see.

"Uh . . . I don't think so. But I hope you get to meet him the next time he comes this way. Charlie's my best friend. I was in his wedding last year."

"That's nice." *Whew.* "So what have you been up to this morning?"

"Not much. It's a beautiful day though. Have you been out yet?"

"I went jogging this morning."

"Why didn't you call me? I would have gone running with you."

"With your bad knees! Are you kidding?" Catherine teased.

What am I doing?

"Oh, you remember that," Clifton responded with a laugh.

"I remember everything you tell me," Catherine replied.

"Hmm. I'll have to watch what I say."

"Too late, I know all the good stuff," she countered. *I have to stop this. This is exactly why I'm not supposed to talk to him.*

She glanced at the clock and wondered if the train Marcus was on had left on time. Reluctantly, she stood up.

"Not all of it," Clifton said, drawing her attention back to him. "There are a few things left that I'd like to tell you, if you'll see me again."

The sensuality in his voice shimmied down between her naked breasts. She was glad that he was not there to see her flush then close her eyes.

"That depends . . . ," she said.

I've got to stop this. He's married.

"I see. Would you consider having brunch with me if I told you my divorce papers came in the mail while I was in LA?"

Catherine's eyes flew open.

"I might," she said, excited. She glanced at the clock again and hoped the train had not left Washington yet.

"Can I come over?"

"I'm expecting to hear from my father . . . How long will it take you to get here?"

"Not long. I'm around the corner, at Frankie's house."

"Pretty sure of yourself, aren't you, Mr. Hayes?"

"No, just wishing and hoping."

Sweetness swelled in Catherine's groin. She could only think of kissing Clifton, touching him and being touched by him, climbing outside her life for just a moment.

"Give me fifteen minutes," she breathed. "But I can only do coffee."

"You got it."

She clinched her fist and pumped it in the air. "Yes!" she shouted. The towel fell off as she danced around the room like an African girl at a celebration of harvest. She fell back on the bed, smiling so hard that her face hurt. Tears of joy formed in the corners of her eyes. "He's divorced," she whispered and wiped them away with the heels of her hands. Suddenly she sat up. "I've got to tell Justine," she said out loud and hurried to the telephone.

The answering machine picked up.

"Justine . . . CALL ME!"

At exactly twelve thirty, the drone of the motor of Clifton's sports car came through the open window. Catherine went to the window and saw the silver Corvette pulling into a parking space. Nervously, she smoothed her hair in place and took one last look at her reflection. She wondered if the highs and lows of the last twenty-four hours showed. There were no signs except for the way the outside corner of her left eye drooped, slightly. She wondered if he would notice. She thought it would not matter to her if he did.

She heard Clifton on the stairs. There was a moment of hesitation between the sound of his last footstep at the top of the landing and his knock on the door. Catherine took a deep breath and opened it.

"Hi, Clifton."

His slow, easy smile spread up to his eyes. They sparkled, and the shine spread like butter to every part of her body.

Without a word, Clifton stepped inside the apartment, closed the door behind him, and opened his arms. Immediately, Catherine stepped into them. She placed her head against his shoulder to feel the warmth of his body. It filled the empty space that had opened up when she'd told him good-bye.

Catherine gently pressed her cheek to his. As she put her arms around his neck, his lips found hers as they kissed. The line where her body ended and his began dissolved. Clifton's hands slid down to Catherine's hips. Suddenly an alarm inside her head went off. *No! This is not right.* She pulled away from him gently and looked up at him and smiled.

"Still not ready?" Clifton said, his eyes searching her face.

"No, it's not that," she lied. "It's just that my dad's coming," she said softly.

Clifton's hands fell to his sides. He shook his head then looked up at the ceiling for a moment as if pleading for mercy. He took a deep breath. "OK."

Catherine placed her hand lightly on his chest and ran it over the smooth material of his shirt, feeling the muscles underneath. Clifton caught her hand and brought her fingers to his lips and kissed them. Then he held it while he reached back and closed the door.

When Catherine returned to the apartment twenty-five minutes later, there were two messages waiting for her: one from her father and one from

Justine. She listened to them both and debated whom to call first. She decided to call Justine.

"Well, someone's in a good mood," Justine said when she heard Catherine's voice. "I was just thinking about you. That was some trip to New York yesterday. What's up?"

"Do you have a minute?" Catherine said, sidestepping the issue that could kill her mood.

"Hold on for a minute while I put the baby down. She's already asleep."

Catherine looked out the kitchen window at the art museum and held on to the joy and contentment Clifton had left her with.

Justine came back. "There. I'm ready."

"Guess who came by." Catherine smiled.

"Hmm. Let me see. Does his name begin with a *C*? Shhh. Don't tell me," Justine teased. "Hmmm . . . Was it Clifton?"

"Uh-huh!" Catherine said. They giggled like schoolgirls. "His divorce has come through."

"No shit!" Justine exclaimed. "That's fabulous. I told you he was one of the good guys."

"Yes, you did."

"So what did the two of you talk about?"

"Mostly, we talked about taking it slow."

"Your need, not his, right?"

"He just got divorced, Justine."

"Oh, come on, Cat. You know I'm right. Just think about it. He's fine, he's smart, he's a gentleman, and he worships the ground you walk on. Harold said you're all he talks about when they play pool."

"Stop making things up, Justine."

"Think what you like, but I saw this coming when he sent you the flowers."

Catherine sighed and surrendered to the flame Justine was fanning. There was no holding her off when it came to men and romance.

Justine went on and on about how Catherine and Clifton were made for each other, the wonderful life they were going to have together, and the pretty babies they were going to make. Catherine's face flushed when Justine mentioned babies, Clifton, and her in the same sentence. She wanted a family, and Mama had told her it would cure her restlessness, her constant need to move from place to place.

"I'll have to get back to you on that," Catherine said. She thought of Marcus waiting for her to call him back.

Her eyes drifted to the calendar and landed on the twelfth of April.

"Chicken!" Justine teased.

"No. Seriously. I have to go," Catherine said. "My dad's waiting to hear from me."

"Remember, you promised to tell him that you haven't heard from Madame Chief. Right?"

"Of course, I'm going to talk to him. But for some reason, I'm feeling better about the anniversary."

"What happened?"

"I don't know . . . Now all I have to do is find out what's going on with Mama. She's going to be so happy when I tell her that I've found someone."

"Well, say hello to your dad for me."

"OK. Ciao, Justine."

Catherine was on her way out when the phone rang. She picked it up, and a sea of static sputtered and crackled loudly in her ear. It was the sound of a bad transatlantic connection.

"Hello? Hello?" she said loudly, on reflex.

The barely audible sound of a woman's voice came through the static. It was scratchy and fractured.

"Hello?" Catherine said again. The static stopped then started up again. Catherine waited for the connection to clear. When it did, she heard something that sounded like two people arguing.

"Hello? Hello?" the caller said through the static. It was Madame Chief. "Catherine . . . Catherine, are you there?"

Catherine's heart leaped high in her chest with excitement.

"Mama, Mama. It's so good to hear from you," she said.

No response. The static created a wall between them.

Catherine fidgeted with the telephone cord, winding it around her pointer finger and unwinding it. She began pacing.

Mama, I'm all right now. I'm sorry about that last letter. I hope you are well. Mama, you'll never guessed what happened today. Mama . . .

The line cleared.

"How are you, daughter?" Madame Chief said.

"Mama, I am well. Mama, how are you?"

"I am . . ."

Dead silence.

Disconnect.

Catherine hung up and stood close to the phone, poised to pick it up the moment it rang. Several minutes passed. She placed her hands on her hips and walked the length of the small kitchen and back again. She stared at the phone as if she could will it to ring again. Nothing! She walked over to the kitchen counter, leaned against it, and tapped on it. She watched the minute hand circling the face of clock on the wall. It seemed to move ever so slowly. A minute passed and then another. It made five more revolutions.

Catherine forced herself to become calm. *She'll call again,* she thought.

Another minute passed. The chance of another call from Africa getting through after a failed connection was fading.

Maybe in an hour or two, she thought. *Mama's probably calling to tell me when she's coming.*

Catherine sighed then picked up her purse and car keys.

"How's everything?" Marcus said as he got in the car.

Catherine leaned over and kissed him on the cheek. "Better." The sands of her life had stopped shifting. "And you?"

She examined the lines in her father's face, noticing that he looked more tired than usual.

"Could be better," Marcus said, avoiding her eyes. He fastened his seat belt.

"Where are we going?" Catherine said.

"It doesn't matter. Where would you like to go?" Marcus replied.

Catherine took another look at the lines on his face and said, "Let's go to the shore."

She pulled into the confluence of traffic circling Swann Fountain, an island of fountains with giant statues of Greek mythical figures in repose that was in the center of the Parkway.

"So what's going on, Dad?" Catherine asked. "More problems with the Nigerian embassy?"

"Nothing we can't handle."

Catherine stole another sideway glance at her father. "How's your stomach holding up?" she inquired.

"Fine," Marcus replied without looking at her. She didn't believe him.

She put on her turn signals and attempted to switch lanes. The driver in the car next to her would not yield the right of way. At the first opportunity, she stepped on the accelerator and pulled ahead of him into the lane.

"Driving in Philly is almost as bad as driving in Lagos," Marcus commented.

She turned onto the ramp to the expressway and the Benjamin Franklin Bridge to Atlantic City, New Jersey. They were there in an hour.

They found a bench and sat facing the ocean. Marcus had become increasingly quiet on the way to the Jersey shore.

"I was wondering if you planned to be in the States on the twelfth. I'm thinking about doing something different this year," Catherine said, looking out at the ocean.

"Like what?" Marcus said, turning to look at her.

"Maybe the three of us can come here this year. I don't think Mama's seen the Atlantic from the Jersey shore. We had planned to come here one year but . . ."

Catherine stopped talking and glanced over at Marcus. He had a faraway look in his eyes.

"Is there something wrong, Dad?"

"I have something to tell you," Marcus said, looking at her. He hesitated.

"Well, what is it?" Catherine said, feeling uneasy.

"Madame Chief has been kidnapped."

"When did that happen?"

Surprised, Marcus stared at her. He had expected something different—shock or fear, not just troubled.

"Dad, what's going on?" Catherine said, her anxiety rising. "You mean *was* kidnapped, don't you?"

"No, she's been missing for four days."

"That's impossible. I just talked to her. She called me before I left my apartment. We didn't have a chance to talk because we were disconnected."

Catherine's eyes scanned her father's face. Fear pooled in her body from her stomach to her throat. Marcus didn't seem convinced.

Marcus stood up quickly. "We have to find a phone."

They went into the first casino hotel they came to.

Catherine's pulse raced as she followed Marcus. They weaved through the crowds in the dim cavernous rooms between rows of glowing slot machines. Bells rang out. Cartoon-like music tinkled everywhere as bets were made. The sound was maddening. They entered a lobby. Seniors out for the day and parents with children moved with molasses-like slowness, slowing them down. To Catherine, their faces were a blur. Finally, they found a phone.

Catherine held her breath while Marcus talked. He stayed on the phone for less than a minute. The look on his face settled the question. Mama was still missing.

The sounds around Catherine died, replaced by a buzzing in her ear. Her brain felt numb. Her legs weakened and threatened to give way. Marcus caught her by the arm. They walked out of the casino and back to the car.

She listened to Marcus as he talked to her as best she could. Marcus tried to comfort her by touching her hand. It was cool and still. He told Catherine what he knew she would want to know—information and details—so that she could make sense of the situation. But the ringing in her ears and the fog in her brain, the slow sinking down into something dark and suffocating, made it difficult to think, let alone understand. Halfway back to Philadelphia, Catherine started having trouble breathing. She reached for the pendant and held it tightly.

"I don't understand, Dad," she managed to say. "How could she call me if rebels have her?"

"They must have found a phone. Someone is helping her."

"Helping her?"

"Apparently, at least one of them wants to help her."

Catherine burst into tears.

Marcus pulled a handkerchief out of the breast pocket of his jacket and handed it to her. She wiped her eyes and stared out the side window, trying to calm down.

"What do they want?"

"No one knows yet."

"Who kidnapped her?"

Silence.

"It's been four days, Dad. Are you telling me that her government still doesn't know that rebel soldiers have her?"

"There's a lot of confusion about that. Sierra Leone government has used their sources in Liberia to find out which of the three rebel groups is responsible for this. They say everyone is pointing the finger at everyone else, and no one can account for the renegade cells."

They crossed the bridge and went back to the Four Seasons. They sat in the parking lot in silence, worlds apart, struggling to stay close.

"Do you want me to come back to your apartment with you?"

"No, not right now. Maybe tomorrow," Catherine said quietly.

"I'm worried about you, Catherine."

"I'll be all right, Dad."

Reluctantly, Marcus said, "OK, I'll call you later." He opened the door.

Catherine looked at him. It was hard to do. She had to work at not letting him see her cry again. *I have to handle my feelings by myself,* she thought. She needed to believe she could because he was leaving in three days and would not be there to take care of her if she started to fall apart.

"Jules is going to be around for a while," Marcus said gently. "He's keeping tabs on the situation. Call him while I'm in Nigeria."

"I'll call him," Catherine said softly.

When she got home, she checked the phone for messages, just in case. There was one from Clifton. She did not call him. Instead, she took a long bath and put on her warmest robe. She drank coffee and played music and curled up on the couch, holding the pillow her Nana Emma had made for her. Her mind played with her, constructing scenarios about the kidnapping and the telephone call. She pictured the place on the road where the rebels stopped Madame Chief. She imaged the rebels, holding a gun to Benjamin's head even though Marcus had not told her this. She imagined them pulling the trigger and blood splattering all over Madame Chief.

"Mama," Catherine called out. Her stomach cramped. She doubled over. Her mouth opened in a soundless cry that took her to a terrible place and began crushing the life out of her. She forced her head up. Air entered her lungs, and she released it in a cry full of misery and pain. She sobbed. "Mama," Catherine cried out. She wrapped her arms around her own trembling body and rocked. She cried and rocked. Rocked and cried. Cried and rocked.

"Mama, Mama, Mama."

Three hours later, her eyes puffy, Nana Emma's pillow stained with tears, Catherine fell asleep.

Marcus called around eleven and woke her up. She told him she was all right. Wearily, Catherine climbed the stairs and went to bed and dreamed of searching the bush for Madame Chief.

CHAPTER SIX

April 3, 2:00 p.m.
Tubmanburg, Liberia

The village had been abandoned for two rainy seasons before they arrived. The hut had parts of the roof torn away. Its walls were speckled with bullet holes. Mohamed sat on a dusty floor with his back resting against a wall. Above his head, there was a hole the size of a baseball. He read his book, a coverless American Western paperback that had yellowed. Fragile pages stuck out precariously. His AK-47 rested on the floor next to him. The straps of his dusty leather sandals lay open, touching the floor.

"Would you stop playing with that gun?" Mohamed snapped, looking up at Blaze through the scratched lens of his reading glasses.

Blaze turned around on the stool and winked at him. Then he returned to the gun and took aim at some fanciful target outside the window. He closed one eye and trained the other down the barrel. Mohamed shook his head and went back to reading.

Blaze cocked the gun. *Click.* He pulled the trigger, and the gun discharged. The bullet hit the limb of a tree at the joint. Quickly, he aimed and fired again, shattering the tree limb with a second bullet before it hit the ground.

Madame Chief opened her eyes momentarily to look at Blaze and closed them again. Her meditation had been disturbed, but she has come to expect this from them. She sat on an armless chair on the other side of the room. She was dressed in a plain cotton robe that had been in the trunk of her car along with her other belongings. Her meal—half of a coconut, a banana, and some wild berries—sat on the makeshift table the rebels built for her after she insisted on having somewhere to place her food other than on the floor where vermin crawled freely. The tabletop was made of branches bound with coarse brown string. It sat unevenly on a tree stump. The fruit sat on a stained piece of cloth. The cloth had been washed many times. Fruit flies had begun to congregate above the food. Mohamed stood up and shooed them away.

There were several more prayers that had to be completed before she was finished. One of them was for Benjamin. He was not with her. The rebels had left him with their comrades in the bush when they crossed over the border into Liberia. She placed her hands' palms down on the miniature New Testament and prayed for his safety.

"That was a good shot," Joe said, rushing into the room. The door was missing. Madame Chief's dress was thrown over one of his shoulders, freeing his hands to hold the unfortunate bird that had been in the tree when the bullet struck it. The bird flapped its wings wildly, struggling to get free. Joe held it tightly by the neck.

"Were you really aiming at the tree, or was it a lucky shot?" he said excitedly. His eyes shone with mischief. He grinned broadly, showing all of his white teeth. Blaze did not answer or look at Joe. He was busy with his gun. He turned it over, examining it from various angles, quickly lifting it to his eye, aiming, lowering it, and aiming again.

Joe looked at Mohamed and eyed his gun.

"What do you want?" Mohamed said, without looking up. He turned another page and eased his hand over to the gun.

"Nothing," Joe said sullenly, eyeing him. He stopped smiling. He walked over to Madame Chief and stood in front of her. Her eyes remained closed for a minute; then she opened them and looked at the dress. Joe had done a fair job of cleaning it. "Hello, Joe," she said and closed her eyes again.

It had become Joe's job to wash Madame Chief's dress in the rivers they came to. He had asked if he could do it because he liked the color and had never touched anything so finely made. This morning, when he went to retrieve it from where he had hung it on a tree limb to dry overnight, he had decided to take a walk. He was restless, tired of waiting for orders to arrive from rebel leaders. The others were also restless.

"How do you like the bird?" Joe said, holding up the exhausted fowl.

He looked at Madame Chief and then at Mohamed to see if they found the bird as fascinating as he did. They didn't. "Too busy, too busy," he said to the bird, referring to them. He shook the bird, agitating it into another wing-flapping frenzy. "OK," he said, looking around. He carried the bird to a cage sitting in a corner. There was a hen already inside. He opened the door, quickly shoved the injured bird inside, and closed the lid before either bird had a chance to escape.

"How do you like that book?" he asked Mohamed on the way back to Madame Chief.

"It is very good," Mohamed said, again without looking up.

Joe sat down cross-legged on the floor in front of Madame Chief. He draped the dress over his head. A minute later, he spun around and sat with his back to her. Then he lifted the skirt just enough to spy on Blaze and the gun. Madame Chief opened her eyes. She stood up, lifted the dress off Joe's head, and went into the other room. Mohamed stood, took off his T-shirt, and covered the hole in the wall.

"What do you think, man? Am I not the best shooter you have ever met?" Blaze said, turning to Joe.

"Let me think on this," Joe said, rubbing his chin. He got up, walked over to Blaze, and stood over him. His eyes traveled from the gun to Blaze and back to the gun. Blaze was staring down the gun barrel at a target outside the window.

"Now I am sure of it. That was a lucky shot. Let me see it," he said, reaching for the AK-47. "I want to try my luck."

"When you tell me what you know is true about my shooting ability, I will let you hold it," Blaze snapped, moving the gun out of Joe's reach.

Joe stepped back and eyed the gun and Blaze, who had again taken aim at something outside the window. A mosquito landed on Blaze's neck. He slapped it and frowned. Joe grinned and lunged for the AK-47. This time he got hold of the gun, but Blaze jerked it away from him with such force that he fell off the stool. His red wig came off his head, but he didn't notice because he was busy kicking at Joe.

"Get away from me, man," Blaze yelled as he scrambled to his feet. He picked up the wig and kept an eye on Joe. Mohamed moved his feet out of the way and continued reading.

Angry, Blaze stepped up to Joe and pushed him hard with his free hand. Joe pedaled backward on his heels, found his balance, then came at Blaze again. They crashed to the floor. Joe reached for the gun, but Blaze kept it out of reach.

"Stop it, man!" Blaze shouted and managed to break free. He got up and stood over Joe, glowering. He pointed the gun at Joe. Joe turned on his back and threw his arms open, laughing. "Not until you give me a try with it," he insisted.

"You are asking for trouble messing with me," Blaze said angrily. Joe jumped to his feet and brushed off his pants and continued to laugh. He set the stool upright and sat on it. "I will take your stool then," he said.

"Fuck you, Joe. It is not my fault you dropped your gun," said Blaze.

"And it is mine? We had to hide and leave when the soldiers came through. I wanted to go back to get it, but you know our new orders are to avoid encounters with the enemy while Mama is traveling with us."

"Whatever the case, man," Blaze countered angrily, "you'll have to wait until we get to the next camp. But maybe you will get lucky. If we run into another unit and have to fight, I will take so many of them down that there will be plenty of guns for you to choose from."

Joe stood up and rubbed his chin as if he was considering what Blaze had said. He walked a few paces away with his head lowered, as if he was thinking. Soon, a sly smile curled the corners of his lips, bringing back the mischievous shine in his eyes that always appeared before he did something that ended up getting him in trouble. He quickly turned and went for Blaze's gun. This time he got it. "What the fuck is wrong with you?" Blaze yelled, reaching for it. Joe pulled the gun away, his finger caught on the trigger. The gun discharged. *Pow!* The bullet cut through the shirt covering the hole in the wall and hit something in the other room. There was a thud.

"Oh shit!" Blaze shouted. Mohamed jumped to his feet, his eyes wide with fear. Joe's jaw dropped. He gaped at the hole, eased the gun down to the floor, and backed away. All three stood frozen in place, terrified. They listened for sound in the other room. Finally, slow footsteps and the rustle of the hem of a skirt sweeping the floor moved toward the door. Madame Chief appeared in the doorway. Glaring, she looked from one to the other.

"Who is responsible for the shot?" she asked. There was no sign of blood on the lime green dress, or the head wrap, or any part of her body that they could see.

From around the corner of the door to the shack, Aaron came into the room. "What has happened here? What was that shooting about?" he demanded. His eyebrows furrowed in a hard line above the rim of his glasses. Fear returned to the boys' faces.

Madame Chief looked down her nose at Aaron, her contempt for him having grown since he separated her from Benjamin, forcing her to become dependent on him. Silently, she turned on her heels and went back into the room.

Aaron looked at the gun lying on the floor.

"What is that doing there?" he said, pointing. "You, come here," he said sternly to Joe.

"It was my fault, Aaron Sir," Joe stammered, not moving.

Aaron's nostrils flared. The veins in his temple throbbed aggressively. He walked over to Joe.

"You are a worthless piece of shit," Aaron growled. He slapped Joe hard across the face, staggering him. "And I am sick of your stupidity. If you were not the nephew of the chief of operations, I would have dumped you in a river a long time ago," he spat, "but if you jeopardize this operation, I won't have to worry about you, will I?"

"I, I . . . ," Joe stammered pathetically.

"Shut up and get out of my sight, all of you," Aaron bellowed, looking from one of the boys to the other. Mohamed and Joe hurried out the door. Blaze stopped to pick up the gun, then left.

Madame Chief sat listening until the commotion had ended; then she stood up and steadied herself on the chair, carefully went to her knees, then rolled onto the mat. Her legs and ankles were swollen again. She rubbed them until they stopped aching. The mat was lumpy. Leaves and twigs had been used to make it. It sat three inches off the floor on tree branches. The rebels had used the rest of the tree to make fires to cook bush meat.

There was one small window in the dark room. A candle sat on a broken plate on the floor near the mat where Madame Chief slept. Mohamed had given her the candle so that she could read her Bible at night.

Madame Chief picked up Catherine's letter, opened it, and read it again. Her heart ached for Catherine. The anniversary of the coup was only nine days away.

My dear daughter, I am so sorry that I cannot be with you, Madame Chief thought and sighed.

She looked around the room, at the bare water-stained walls with gaping holes and missing plaster. The newest bullet hole, made by Joe just moments ago, was in the wall behind her. Mohamed and Joe had cleared the room of old mattresses and dirty rags and swept the room clean of insects with brooms made of twigs tied together. But there was nothing they could do to get rid of the strong musty odor caused by the mold. Suddenly, Madame Chief felt tired. The excitement of having nearly been shot had exhausted her. "Lord, God, Father. See me through this," she whispered.

She had attempted to contact Catherine the day the soldiers stopped in Vionjama at a house belonging to a Lebanese couple, a wealthy businessman and his wife. The couple had an arrangement with the leaders of the LRFD. They were willing to give the rebels food, all they could eat and carry with them, in exchange for not ransacking the house. Mohamed had talked the woman into letting Madame Chief use her phone, the only working phone in a thirty-mile radius. Aaron had walked in on Madame Chief while she was talking to Catherine. The Lebanese woman had taken offense to his demand that Madame Chief hang up. They argued. Aaron pulled the cord out of the wall and wrapped it around her neck. He stopped short of killing her, but he warned Madame Chief, "If you try that again, you will have this woman's death on your conscience."

I will find a way to get a message to her, Madame Chief thought. *She must know that God and the ancestors have been with us each year at the memorial site, and they will be there whether or not I am there. Or did I fail to communicate that to her?*

Madame Chief turned on her side. She was sleepy but afraid to close her eyes. Recently, she'd had dreams about death. *Maybe my time on this earth is coming to an end,* she thought.

She surveyed the dismal space and remembered her bedroom with its comfortable four-poster, mosquito netting, lemon-colored muslin curtains, and large windows. It faced the ocean. Every day the Atlantic breezes swept through and carried out the odor of mold.

A small lizard scurried across the floor close to the mat. She stretched out her hand to block its path. Its reflexes were sharp. It turned quickly to avoid her, then scurried into a corner and up the wall a few feet. Madame Chief smiled, entertained by the agility of the creature that she had not played with since she was a little girl.

Someone had left a page from a newspaper pinned to the wall. The ink and images had faded. Madame Chief wondered who had put it there and why it had been important enough to hang up. It caused her to think about the picture of her father hanging on the wall of her bedroom.

The frame was oval shaped and made of dark wood. The black-and-white photo had been taken around the turn of the century. His small wiry body was dressed in full regalia. His skin was black. His eyes were penetrating and inquiring, his expression both suspicious of the camera and impatient with the amount of time it was taking the photographer to set up. Madame Chief sighed and longed to talk to him. The swelling in her legs became a dull ache. She thought about what the boys had told her. They were trying to find a doctor for her. She needed medicine. They had made an earnest attempt as far as she could see. The doctor that they brought to her the night before did not have the medicine she needed. They said they could not to take her back to Sierra Leone in her condition because it would "cause too many problems."

Still what was their mission? What did it have to do with her? How did she fit into it? When she questioned Aaron about when they planned to take her home, he was evasive, and she was left with the impression that he was stalling. Mohamed had let it slip that his comrades were still holding Benjamin. Why?

Whenever she was not trying to figure out what the rebels were up to, she thought about Catherine and the events that caused her to forget to write to say she was not coming to America.

She was on the way down the stairs to take afternoon tea in the library when unexpected visitors had arrived in the compound. She'd stopped at the foot of the stairs to study the two men getting out of a jeep.

David Banjo worked for Minister Fofana in the Office of Minerals and Natural Resources. Of average height and a slight build, he looked older than his thirty years. Like most African men in Sierra Leone, his hair was cut close, his face was smooth, and the whites of his eyes were yellowish. He was dressed in a pressed tan political suit. He carried himself as if he was certain of his importance.

The other man was Jim Finnegan. Jim looked around the compound as if he owned it. His legs were white and hairy, but his arms and neck were lobster red. He wore khaki shorts, a white shirt, and hiking boots that were covered with dust and dried mud. David had looked past Jim, nervously keeping a watchful eye on the door to Madame Chief's house, fully expecting a servant to come out to query him about his reason for coming to see Madame Chief without an appointment.

Though appointments with her were difficult to arrange, visitors rarely came to see her without one. The usual practice was to send a courier to her house to make arrangements because there were no telephone wires to connect the village to the city. It took a full day to drive from Freetown to her house in Mokebe, over roads where miles of asphalt had been washed away exposing rough hard dirt and jagged stone.

The unscheduled visit struck Madame Chief as an intentional breach of protocol, but it was not the worst of what would come her way.

Madame Chief had seen Jim before in the lobby of the Hotel Bintumani several months earlier. Now he was standing in front of her house. Coincidence?

When she stepped out on the porch, Madame Chief surmised that Jim had not expected to see her so quickly. He had looked at David with a question on his face. David's expression was blank. Then for some reason known only to him, Jim had grinned as if amused. He turned, and with his hat held against his chest, he came toward her. He stopped three feet from the porch, squinting at her with pale blue eyes.

Madame Chief had not been impressed with his show of deference. It seemed contrived, as if Jim thought he knew how to relate to someone of her station. Obviously he had not. He had not dressed properly to see her. He was dressed to go on safari, not visit a paramount chief. He was as transparent as glass to her and did not even know it. Still, Madame Chief was curious about him. Later, she would regret that she had not sent them both away.

"What is your name?" Madame Chief asked.

"Jim Finnagan, ma'am," he responded with a thick drawl.

"Where are you from?"

"Houston, Texas, ma'am."

His informal behavior had made her uneasy in a way she could not put her finger on. He started to say something else, but Madame Chief put up her hand, cutting him off. She went back in the house and continued to the library.

Soon another truck had arrived. Madame Chief observed it from a window.

There were four men sitting in the open back of the truck with bandanas around their noses and mouths. Dust covered their hair and clothes. They were slumped over, exhausted from the 110 degree heat. Madame Chief had recognized one of them. His name was Kaloko. No one had seen him in over a year. There had been rumors about him, though none of them good. The one that seemed most plausible was that Kaloko had been forced to join the rebels.

There had been four such abductions since the last time anyone had seen him. Madame Chief's heart filled with happiness when she saw that Kaloko was alive and that he had found work.

A third truck arrived, army issue.

Ester, her head maid of nineteen years and second most trusted servant, had come in and gone straight to the window. Ester was tall, large framed, and plain. She rarely smiled.

"Why has David come to the village today?" she muttered.

A second later Nadia, Madame Chief's personal maid who never strayed far from her side, came up behind them to watch the scene in the courtyard. Petite, with beautiful, ever-watchful large eyes, she'd searched Madame Chief's house periodically looking for juju objects—"bad magic"—that mysteriously showed up from time to time. She'd found the last one within days of David and Jim's arrival—a stick smeared with tree sap and bird feathers in a box under Madame Chief's bed. Nadia had buried it deep in the bush and mentioned it to no one.

"Nadia, go to the covered truck and look inside. I want to know what is in it," Madame Chief had said to her.

David's expression had remained blank while Nadia looked in the truck, but Jim had smirked, leaving Madame Chief to wonder what game they were playing. When Nadia came back, she said, "Mama, there be machines there. I see this before when the men come to dig the mines in my old village."

"Are you positive?" Madame Chief said baffled.

"Oh yes, Mama. I be absolutely sure."

Now, Madame Chief's instinct had been aroused, but it was overruled by her head and the need to know what had brought David and Jim to her fishing village.

"Tell David to come to the library."

David stood at the door, waiting while Madame Chief went over various domestic concerns with Ester. It was his first time in her library. Enthralled, he'd looked around at the paintings on the walls, the collection of folk art from around the world, the ornately carved legs and feet on the furniture, and the books that were everywhere—on shelves, in corners, and under tables.

"Sit down, David," Madame Chief had said, turning to him and motioning to the sofa. She took a seat in a wingback chair and studied him. David's nervousness was evident in his eyes. They were wide and unblinking. "Mama, please excuse the intrusion on your day," he said.

He carried a large manila envelope. He placed it on the seat next to him, pulled it close to his leg, and protectively laid his hand on it. Madame Chief noticed the gold watch he was wearing. His eyes followed hers. She had heard that he had been promoted to permanent secretary. With this new position, he could buy the new suit he was wearing that day and feed his family without struggling, but the gold watch was an extravagance that exceeded his means.

"How are your children and your wife?" she inquired, ignoring his apology and challenging its sincerity. David shifted almost imperceptibly in his seat, but the slight movement did not escape her.

"Thanks be to Allah, they are well."

"And your mother and father?"

"They are also in good health, Mama."

Ester returned to the room carrying a tray with several cups, a pitcher of water, and two glasses.

"May I offer you tea, or would you prefer water?" Madame Chief had asked, taking as much time as she needed to continue sizing David up.

"Water please, Mama," David responded.

His hand shook slightly when he took the glass of water from Ester. Madame Chief had pretended not to notice.

"It is a beautiful day for a long ride, is it not?" Madame Chief said.

"Yes, Mama."

"And you are on your way to . . . ?"

"Only to see you, Mama."

"I see . . ."

Ester handed Madame Chief a glass of water.

"Will you have tea also, Mama?" Ester had asked Madame Chief.

"Yes, Ester."

Unhurried, Ester poured a cup of tea then cut her eyes at David.

David had shifted in the chair and had taken a furtive glance at Ester and at Madame Chief. Madame Chief found his uneasiness with Ester curious.

David's eyes had followed Ester until she left the room. He contemplated the glass of water in his hand until the echo of her footsteps had died. Madame Chief looked at him and saw the little boy who often broke the rules when he played soccer. David had always been ambitious.

"Tell me, David, what brings you to my village today? Is your business so pressing that you found it necessary to come to see me without an appointment?"

"I apologize for not making an appointment in advance," David said.

"That's quite all right, David."

"I have a letter for you from Minister Fofana. He wanted you to receive it as soon as possible." He opened the envelope. "It will explain everything."

Minister Fofana was a shrewd businessman with great investment acumen. Madame Chief had often thought it egregious that a man with his skills and intelligence was not busy figuring out a way to save Sierra Leone from drowning in debt. There was also tribal enmity between them. Minister Fofana was Temne, and Madame Chief was Mende.

Someone has misled Abraham if he thinks there is something of value in my little fishing village, *she thought.*

The letter had informed her that Jim Finnagan was a land surveyor and that he was there on an "exploratory mission and should be extended your full courtesy."

She'd bristled at that line.

Minister Fofana is acting above himself.

The letter read,

Mr. Finnagan has agreed to stay in Sierra Leone and go forward with excavations. If there is evidence that something of interest to the ministry is found, he will report it directly to the Ministry of Minerals and Natural Resources, and that information will subsequently be passed on to you.

Respectfully,
Minister Abraham Fofana,
Minister of Minerals and Natural Resources

There was a line for her signature. She had stared at it speechless.

"Where is the rest of the letter, David?" she'd demanded, indignant.

David blinked once. "That is all there is, Mama."

She'd watched as he turned the glass up high and gulped down the water. Then she turned the page over and looked at the other side as if something more should be written there. She'd studied the minister's signature expecting to see something in the slope or curve of the letters that might explain his attitude. She'd fingered the bond lightly to determine if the letter had come from his office. The quality was too fine, characters too crisp and clear. It was evident that the letter had been typed somewhere else.

She'd looked up to find David staring at her. On reflex, he had looked away and drank the last of the water.

Again, Madame Chief had studied the line drawn for her signature giving David permission to complete the survey. Dumbfounded, she placed it on the table, stood up, and went to the window. The decision she was about to make was serious. Fofana had the upper hand.

No one had ever dared to use coercion with her, though there were many men who boldly and openly expressed dislike of women in authority. Her tribe was one of few that allowed power to be passed down to women. There had only been one other woman to ever hold the position of paramount chief. Fofana's message was clear: Do not challenge me!

I need time to think about this, *Madame Chief had thought as an indescribable tiredness came over her.*

"This is not a good day for the village to have visitors," she said, turning to David. "I will send someone to inform Minister Fofana when Jim Finnagan can return. Have a safe journey back to Freetown, David." She left the room.

The next day, another bureaucrat of the ministry had come to see her unannounced. His position in the department was lower than David's. He'd nervously smoked one cigarette after the other and was as vague and evasive as David had been. He left without her signature.

A week later, another civil servant, a file clerk, had come to her house with the letter. Nadia met him at the door and informed him that Madame Chief was taking a nap. He said he would wait and found a tree to sit under and doze. When Madame Chief woke up several hours later, she'd frowned and gone back to her room when she learned who Minister Fofana had sent. It was clear that Fofana intended to disrespect and minimize her, to aggravate her into reconsidering her position.

Nadia had advised the file clerk to go back to Freetown before the sun set, but he said he would wait until Mama had time to see him. He went back to the tree and dozed off. That night, he curled up in the backseat of the old rusting car that he had arrived in and went to sleep. The next morning, one of the servants had given him breakfast and asked him to leave.

Every day for the next two weeks, someone from the ministry had come with the letter. Each one held a lower rank in the ministry than the one before, until finally it was not possible to find anyone lower.

Night had fallen by the time Madame Chief awoke. Feeling better, she sat up. Sleep had been peaceful and satisfying. She was grateful. The next room was still.

"Mohamed? Joe? Blaze?"

Silence enveloped Madame Chief. The pungent odor of burning wood drifted in the room through the window. She called the rebels again.

In the days since being kidnapped, she had developed some affection for all the rebels but Aaron. She saw a difference between his desire to draw blood from his enemies and the things Blaze did. Blaze had told her that when he was fourteen, a brutal rebel leader had used mind control and drugs on him and other teenagers they had recruited. They quickly became addicted to these powerful psychologically destabilizing drugs—cannabis sprinkled with gun powder and palm oil and cocaine mixed with gun powder. The bra and wig became part of Blaze's uniform one night when he and these boys, now his friends and comrades, were ordered to drive into downtown Monrovia and shoot everyone in sight. They had been smoking and sniffing the drugs for several hours. Their car went out of control, and they had crashed through the window of a women's shop, jumped out, and trashed the store. When they came out, they were wearing wigs and bras. Soldiers of the existing government were waiting for them, but somehow Blaze and the other boys escaped the hail of bullets and drove out of town unscratched. "I forgive you," Madame Chief had said. "Your good sense has left you because of what was done to you and what you have done. But you must stop using the drugs," she warned.

Aaron's brutality, on the other hand, was not forgivable. He never touched drugs, but his appetite for violence and spilled blood disturbed her at her core.

Once while traveling to a new camp, they had stumbled on rebels loyal to Prince Johnson, the rival rebel leader who controlled the northern territories of Liberia. The men were no match for Aaron and Blaze. They thought they had killed all nine of them. However, while collecting their guns and ammunition, one of the rebels rose up and cut Aaron's leg. Aaron had turned on the man and plunged a knife into his chest and stomach, working it to eviscerate him. He did not bother to wipe the blood from his hands before taking a gun and riddling the dead man's body with bullets. It did not seem to matter to Aaron that Madame Chief had witnessed his crime. He smiled at Blaze, then made sure she was watching as he kicked the dead rebel's head.

"Madame, you called?" Mohamed suddenly appeared in the doorway, holding a candle.

"Oh, Mohamed," Madame Chief said startled. She placed a hand over her heart. "Please do not come to me like that again," she said gently but firmly.

"Mama, I am sorry," Mohamed apologized. "We heard you call."

Blaze and Joe appeared in the door behind Mohamed.

"Help me to my feet."

"A rebel friend came with new orders, and we talked to him about what was happening in Monrovia," Joe said as they helped her stand up. "We are leaving here in the morning and going to meet up with the others. He said some of us have been fighting Charles Taylor's soldiers. We are also fighting Prince Johnson's rebels who want to take control of Monrovia. He didn't stay long. He had other stops to make, and he wanted to get back quickly."

Joe's eyes twinkled, and he grinned from ear to ear.

"He had three notes with the names written on the front. I asked him if he was sure that he was giving me the right one. He laughed and said they all said the same thing—that it did not matter, and he was sure I had the one for Aaron Sir. I cannot read very good, but Mohamed is teaching me the alphabet. I remembered the letters on the envelope."

"Tell me what the letters were," said Madame Chief.

"A-a-r-o-n F-o-f-a-n-a."

CHAPTER SEVEN

April 4, 1:00 p.m.
Philadelphia, Pennsylvania

Justine was sitting in the car, flipping through a magazine, when Catherine came out. She threw the magazine on the backseat on top of a pile of toys, furry animals, coloring books, and half-empty boxes of broken crayons.

"Hey." Justine scanned what she could see of Catherine's face behind the large oversized sunglasses she was wearing.

"Hi," Catherine said, not smiling.

She got in and snapped the seat belt in place. Justine reached for her hand and squeezed it gently.

"How about let's go somewhere quiet?"

Catherine nodded.

They came to Fairmount Avenue. The street dead-ended there, perpendicular to the old abandoned Eastern State Penitentiary that had been renovated into a tourist attraction. A tour bus pulled up beside them. Passengers craned their necks at the prison to get a better look and snapped pictures. Catherine stared at the prison's immense stone wall. It reflected the wall that was forming around her. Her mood was somber, like someone who had just come from a funeral. She was dressed accordingly in a black turtleneck, skirt, jacket, and heels.

Justine had cut her hair into a short pixie style. Large curls crowned her head and tapered feather-like down the nape of her neck. Catherine noticed but could not muster enough interest to ask Justine about her new hairdo.

They took the expressway out of town and headed toward the suburbs. Justine filled the air with small talk, attempting to break through the wall of silence surrounding Catherine.

"Wait 'til you have kids," she remarked out of the blue. "You'll see how hard it is to stay at home and not talk to another adult all day. By the way, did I mention that I talked to my old boss about coming back to work part-time?"

Catherine lowered her glasses and looked over the rim at Justine. Justine had not talked about going back to work in nearly three years, not since before her last daughter was born.

The year after Justine had graduated summa cum laude from Georgetown, she went straight to New York, and within months, she had landed a job in an advertising agency in an office in downtown Manhattan. That same year, she met Harold Carpenter who was in his third year of residency. A year later they were married, and three months later, Justine was pregnant.

"So that's why you cut your hair," Catherine said, replacing her shades and leaning back against the seat, staring ahead at the road.

"One of the reasons."

"There's another?"

"Boredom for one."

Catherine looked out the side window.

"So what do you think about that?" Justine said, glancing over at her.

"I think it's great," Catherine said quietly. "What does Harold think about it?"

"He flipped, of course. He still insists that Sonya should start kindergarten before I go back to work."

A year ago, Catherine had sent Justine a Senegalese au pair so that Justine could go back to work whenever she was ready. Catherine had known the girl since the girl was five years old. She was a gentle girl, the kind of girl Justine would feel comfortable leaving her children with. Harold had rejected the girl outright. Since she spoke little English, he'd sent her back to Catherine with a note saying, "Mind your own business, Cat."

"I feel guilty enough as it is," Justine said, getting back to the first thing on her list of things to talk to Catherine about.

"About what?" Catherine asked.

"About wanting to go back to work. You know the girls are the center of my universe, but I'm seriously understimulated and my brain is oversaturated with mother's milk." She laughed nervously.

"What?" Catherine said, staring at her. "I didn't get the part about mother's milk."

"Yesterday, I woke up thinking it was time to nurse Sonya."

"It's definitely time for you to go back to work," Catherine said, perking up a little. "Let Harold stay home with Sonya until she's old enough to go to school. We'll see what he thinks about hiring somebody then."

"Did I mention that I have a date to get my tubes tied in May?"

Catherine looked over at Justine. Justine tried to smile, but it froze into a grimace.

"Let me know when you have a firm date. I'll take care of the girls for you," Catherine offered.

Justine had confessed to Catherine that she had had an abortion. She had been too ashamed to tell her at the time, and she still felt tortured by the decision. Having her tubes tied was something she believed she had to do, the only surefire way to stop having babies. Birth control pills tended to make her sick, and the rhythm method was too chancy. She had made Catherine promise to watch over her daughters if anything happened to her while she was under anesthesia. Catherine had assured Justine that nothing would happen to her, but for good measure, she had asked Mama to pray for Justine.

"Feeling better?" Justine said, glancing over at Catherine.

"Not really," Catherine replied.

"Do you want to talk now?"

"Maybe later," Catherine said, staring straight ahead.

"Talk to me, Cat," Justine urged.

"I can't right now."

"Why did you call if we aren't going to talk?" Justine muttered under her breath.

"What did you say?"

"Nothing."

Catherine turned on the radio and fiddled with the dial until she found an R&B station. She settled back in the seat.

"Liberian rebels took Mama," she said.

"Why?" Justine blurted out, shocked.

"No one seems to know."

"I don't understand. Why would Liberian rebels kidnap her? Doesn't she live in Sierra Leone?

"Sierra Leone and Liberia share a border. It's as easy for rebels to get into Sierra Leone as it is for Mexicans to cross the border into the United States. Probably easier because members of the same tribe live on both sides."

"What do they want? Money?"

"The rebels do crazy things. Who knows what they want, or if they want anything at all."

"So they just take people?"

"Not usually. Usually, they maim and kill them and take their food," Catherine replied.

Justine's mouth dropped open. Recovering, she said, "This is unbelievable, Cat. What's her government doing about it?"

"Not enough. If things were different, Sierra Leone and Liberian soldiers would be fighting at the border by now. Under no circumstances would this have been tolerated this long. Charles Taylor is holding on to Liberia, but the country doesn't have a solid government or army. There's no one to charge with the crime."

"Come again?"

"There are at least three rebel groups fighting Charles Taylor and each other for control of Liberia, and new ones keep forming almost overnight."

"Prince Johnson's rebels and what's his name, Roosevelt somebody? Right?"

Catherine looked at Justine, surprised that she had been paying attention to anything she had told her about Liberia. Justine had not expressed interest in politics.

"No one knows," Catherine replied.

"There must be something that can be done," Justine insisted.

"There is. The UN and the international community will try to work through diplomatic channels but . . ."

"But what?" Justine said.

"Nothing."

"What is it?"

"Sometimes we use the CIA."

"The CIA?" Justine's eyes stretched wide. "Why can't President Taylor do something?"

Catherine looked troubled. "Taylor makes people in international circles uneasy. He's not someone you want to owe a favor."

"How about your father?"

Catherine fell silent. "He'll do what he can," she said after a moment. She turned and stared out the window.

"Are you OK?"

"Why?"

"You have a funny look on your face."

"I'll be fine."

Justine hesitated. "Do you think she's OK?"

Catherine did not answer. A knot stuck in her throat. They drove in silence for a few minutes.

"I wish I knew more about Madame Chief," said Justine.

"Why now?"

"I guess I'm surprised you called me instead of one of your other friends. You know, someone who really understands what this kidnapping means over there in Africa."

Catherine reflected on how no one who had been working at the embassy the night the marines brought her back had wanted to talk to her about what had happened. They still avoided it in one way or another, saying, "Let the past be the past." She was absolutely certain they wouldn't want to talk to her about this either. *It's too much like history repeating itself, or lighting striking me twice. No one's going to touch this,* she'd thought before deciding to call Justine.

"There is no one else to talk to about this, Justine."

Surprised, Justine looked over at Catherine. Catherine realized that Justine could not understand the gravity of Mama's abduction. She was American. But she was glad Justine had finally asked her about Madame Chief. It made her feel less alone.

Catherine started with Madame Chief's career in the UN. "She's recognized by the UN as the voice for women in Africa. She's held several important positions. After her father died, she campaigned to be elected paramount chief of Mokebe and won it easily because the majority of her subchiefs supported her."

Catherine lapsed into thought for a few moments then continued. "Being a female paramount chief is hard. Mama is only the second woman voted into office. There are so many things Mama has tried to change . . . She spoke out against female circumcision at the women's conference in China during the Year of the Woman and tore the cover off a ritual that had gone uncensored for ages. There were threats on her life that year. It passed though. I think that Mama has depended on her high visibility to discourage retaliation. Her enemies try to get to her through the members of her household. They have been either threatened or coerced into trying to sabotage Mama. It bothers me that juju is found in her house. But the person who puts it there is always found out. Something like kidnapping her is, or was, inconceivable. It's a stupid move. If she's not brought back soon, it would cause a war. Many African men in power resent her influence. The people love her, but more importantly, they need her. Their national identity is threatened when she is not safe. I believe some people would say that Sierra Leone's survival is at risk. She carries the wealth of their heritage by simply being . . ."

Fatigued, Catherine stopped. The heaviness in her chest had increased with every word she had spoken about Mama until the effort became insufferable.

They drove in silence for several minutes.

"How's your dad?" Justine asked.

"He's OK."

"When's he going back to Africa?"

"Soon." Catherine watched a drift of clouds headed in her direction.

"Where's he going?"

"Nigeria."

After a moment's hesitation, Justine said, "I was wondering if your dad will be around to go with you out to the farm this year."

"No, he can't. Besides, I wasn't planning to go out there this year."

"Are you OK with your dad being away?" Justine pressed.

"If you had asked me that a couple days ago, I would have said yes. Now I'm not sure."

Catherine turned away and stared at the sky. It was getting dark.

"What about your friend Jules. Have you talked to him lately?"

"I talked to him a couple days ago. He's next on my list," said Catherine. "If anyone knows what's going on in Sierra Leone, he does. I'm pissed off with him though."

"How come?"

"He knew she was missing when I talked to him the day before he left Sierra Leone."

"You know it wasn't his place to tell you, Cat."

Catherine's face hardened. "I could have been a little ahead of the game if I had known earlier."

"What do you mean by that?"

Catherine turned away and looked up at the sky. A heavy rain began to fall.

CHAPTER EIGHT

April 5
Philadelphia

"Well, look who's come to visit," Catherine said when Jules walked through the door of her apartment. Jules ignored her snide remark. He was expecting it. He kissed her on the cheek.

Overnight, Catherine's mood had changed from solemn to angry. Marcus had left her hanging, and she had talked to a friend who had given her discouraging news about Sierra Leone.

Now on his way to Nigeria, Marcus had assured Catherine that he would look into Madame Chief's situation. This meant he had already talked to the State Department and others who were also concerned. "Maybe I should go to Sierra Leone," she had responded. "You're tied up with Nigeria, and Jules doesn't have the time to give this his full attention."

"Sit tight, baby. Give it a few more days," Marcus had replied, concerned about the direction Catherine's thoughts were taking. "When I see President Obasanjo, I'll discuss the problem with him." Catherine agreed to wait until she heard from Marcus because he had planned to ask the Nigerians for help. Then she ran into Heribert Bangura outside a coffee shop near the university. Justine had just dropped her off so she could check on an art delivery that had arrived. Heribert had stopped by the campus to talk to one of his former professors. Heribert had told Catherine that the word on the street was that Madame Chief's kidnappers had been identified.

"The men in Mama's village were preparing to go look for her when President Payne sent soldiers to close the border, to stop the rebels from preying on the border villages. The soldiers and rebels fight every day now. No one is safe crossing from either side. Things are getting bad in Sierra Leone, and my wife and I have talked seriously about moving. We may go to England. She has family there, and they can help me find a teaching job. We're not certain yet."

Catherine hadn't asked him to elaborate on what he meant by "things." She didn't want to know.

Jules followed Catherine in the kitchen and took a seat at the table. "How about a cup of coffee?"

"Coffee huh?" Catherine responded. "This had better not be a 'let me calm Catherine down' visit," she warned.

"Your dad's given me the green light to keep you posted, little sister," Jules said.

"Yes, but you haven't been exactly swift about it, have you?"

"What makes you think that? When I get it, you get it."

"So why am I the last person to find out that Mama's kidnappers have been identified?"

She put the cup of coffee down on the table in front of Jules and stood over him with her hands on her hips.

"I just found out about it myself," he said, leaning back in the chair and looking up at her. "Sit down. You make me nervous when you stand over me like that."

Catherine went back to the counter and poured another cup of coffee. She leaned on the counter and eyed Jules.

"OK, I found out yesterday. I didn't call you because I was planning to stop by this morning," he said.

"Don't bullshit me, Jules."

"Hold tight, Catherine. We're on it. Besides, I wanted to talk to a few people before I called you," he said casually, trying to loosen Catherine up. "Would you come over here and sit down, please?"

He pulled out a chair and motioned to it.

"And what did you find out?" she said before sitting.

"Tell me what you know first."

Catherine sat down and told Jules everything Heribert had told her.

"Well, that's about the size of it, except that one of our sources believes that the rebels are taking very good care of Madame Chief."

"Is the source reliable?"

"Reliable enough. I don't have all the details yet, but I think we can trust it."

The source Jules was referring to was the doctor who had treated Madame Chief. Jules decided to not tell Catherine the part about Madame Chief's heart problem.

"I also talked to a UN rep who said he would work on it from his end."

"That's it?"

"For now."

Catherine looked out the window and fell silent.

"Jules," Catherine said, turning to him, "I don't like this."

"Don't worry. We're on this."

"Please don't," Catherine said, holding up one hand in protest.

"You have to calm down, Catherine."

"Why?" She turned and stared straight at Jules.

"Because we're making progress. It will be handled, trust me."

"Don't try to convince me that everything's under control. You know I know better than that."

"I'm not trying to convince you of anything, Catherine," Jules said, unwilling to yield his position. "A lot of people are going to work on this issue. We *are* going to get her back home safely."

Catherine was moved by Jules's resolve. She wanted to believe him, but something inside her resisted.

Jules looked at his watch. "I have to go," he said, standing. "I'll keep in touch."

"Promise me one thing," said Catherine. "If anything bad happens to Mama, I won't have to hear it from someone else."

"The minute anything changes, I'll call you," he replied and kissed Catherine on the cheek.

* * *

Later that evening, Catherine sat on the sofa holding Nana Emma's pillow, watching television. Her mind was beginning to clear on the subject of going to Sierra Leone.

She was less angry, but she could not shake her anxiety about the rebels holding Madame Chief. She forced herself to concentrate on what Jules had told her, that the rebels were taking care of Mama, but she wanted—no, needed—to know that they planned to bring Madame Chief back to her village very soon. *They realized they made a mistake.* The thought helped her feel a little less desperate, but she could not convince herself that they could behave rationally. That was too much to expect. And then there was the matter of the upcoming anniversary on April 12. It terrified her to think that it was possible for fate to mock her and Mama by throwing her back into the living hell she had found her way out of, almost. Déjà vu? *Not now, please not now.*

Suddenly Catherine thought how incredible it would be if she went to Africa during the month of April. It would be the first time in twelve years that she had visited an African country so close to the anniversary.

Can I do this? Isn't it time?

A knot formed in her stomach. She sat up and turned on the Public Broadcasting Service at six o'clock to watch the evening news. A report on the refugee camps in Sierra Leone came on.

She had seen the camps up close: the relief workers talking about the dire conditions; the refugees wearing sad expressions; men, women, and children in dirty clothes. Missing from the television report was the smell of body odor, human waste, and death. Also missing were scenes of people huddled in groups being taught to read by a missionary or praying.

The program was followed by a detailed report of a proposed meeting between the leaders of the African countries, the Economic Community of West African States, its military arm, ECOMOG, and the UN. They were prepared to send peacekeeping troops to Liberia. The talks were progressing.

When the program ended, she prepared her dinner then picked at it while listening to Marvin Gaye sing "What's Going On?" Suddenly feeling restless, she thought about going out. Where? For no reason in particular, at least none that she could determine, Clifton popped into her head. She had not spoken to him since finding out about Madame Chief. He had left messages, but she had not returned one call. She was not sure what to say to him, how much to tell him about Mama, Sierra Leone, Liberia, her life before he came along. He was aware that she had lived in Africa and had ties there but not more than that. She decided to call him and play it by ear.

"Hello?"

"Hi."

"Catherine. It's nice to hear from you." She could hear the surprise in his voice.

"Do you have a minute?"

"I always have time for you."

"I guess you're wondering why I haven't returned your calls."

"I thought you were getting cold feet again."

"No. Something came up. I've been preoccupied."

"Is everything all right?"

Catherine sidestepped the question.

"I'm thinking about going to Africa."

"For how long?"

"I'm not sure. Maybe a week or so."

"When are you leaving?"

"As soon as I can get a visa."

Silence.

Clifton cleared his throat. "Can I see you before you go?"

"I don't know. I . . ."

"Catherine?"

"Yes."

"I need to see you before you go."

Don't let him push you into anything Catherine.

"I have to go to work early tomorrow."

"So do I. I won't keep you long. I just have a feeling that if I don't see you tonight, I may not see you for a while."

He's right.

"Meet me at Gloria's."

"I'll be there."

CHAPTER NINE

April 8
Philadelphia

Catherine's eyes followed a plane flying overhead. Justine's youngest daughter, Sonya, had fallen asleep in her lap. She buried her nose in the baby's soft hair and reflected on the pained expression that had passed over Justine's face when she told her she was leaving for Sierra Leone in two days.

Justine came back from the playground area where she had retreated after Catherine gave her the news. She sat down, turned to Patrice and Naomi, her other daughters, and pointed a finger at them. "Now, remember what I told you. No more fighting." They looked at her and frowned. She frowned as well.

Justine's middle child, Patrice, had her father's complexion, brown with a reddish tinge. Her thick hair was braided into two braids. Naomi, the oldest, looked like Justine. She was tall for seven years old.

"I don't know what's got into them lately! I can't leave them alone for a minute," Justine said, flustered.

"Oh, they're OK." Catherine looked in their direction. They were already up running around the slide, laughing and grabbing each other.

"I suppose so," Justine replied, rubbing one of her bare arms, a sign that she was worried.

"How's my pumpkin?" Justine leaned over and peered at Sonya's face. She brushed Sonya's cheek with the back of her hand.

"She's fine. Nothing bothers her, does it?" said Catherine.

"Not much. She's my easy child right now."

Sonya woke up and looked around, dazed. Her cheeks were flushed. Her eyes widened when she spotted Justine. She leaned forward, wiggling her small plump fingers.

"OK, pumpkin," Justine said, gently lifting Sonya up into her arms. Sonya laid her head against Justine's shoulder, stuck a thumb in her mouth, and drifted back off to sleep.

"How are you doing?" Justine asked Catherine.

"I'm fine right now," Catherine replied.

Silence.

"What are you going to do when you get to Sierra Leone? Sit around?" Justine sounded irritated.

"Not exactly," Catherine evaded.

"Why don't you just wait until you hear from your dad?"

"I've waited long enough. Besides, you know I always see Mama on the twelfth. Obviously, she's not going to get here in time, so I'm going there. What's the big deal?" Catherine turned to study Justine's face.

Justine was frowning again.

"What's wrong, Justine?"

"Nothing," Justine said. She picked up Sonya's hand and gently rubbed her fingers. Suddenly her face clouded. "If you really want to know, this whole thing is pissing me off!"

I don't need this, Catherine thought, turning away and fighting the urge to get up and walk off.

Sonya grumbled in her sleep and squirmed uncomfortably.

"Cat, can I ask you something?" Justine said, rocking Sonya and looking intently at Catherine.

"What is it?"

"Aren't you afraid of Africa just a little bit?"

Puzzled, Catherine turned back to Justine.

"I know you go there all the time but . . . Well . . . I suppose if I had gone through what you went through, I'd have some reservations about going back there," Justine said.

"Oh I see. You think I should have been finished with Africa after that," said Catherine. "When did you begin to think that?"

"I've always thought that, and even more so now that I talked to one of your friends at the reception."

Justine paused to study Catherine's face. Another plane passed overhead. Catherine looked up.

"I really wish you would consider putting off the trip for a while, at least until after the anniversary. I've been thinking a lot about what happened to you," she continued, carefully choosing her words. "It all makes sense now, the way you change every spring. You never go to Africa at this time of the year. I hadn't put that together before. The twelfth is only a few days away. Why don't you wait?"

Catherine took a deep breath and looked away and stared into space. The anniversary was only four days away. Just like clockwork, dreams about the night of the coup had begun. They were somewhat less frightening, though. In these dreams, she didn't fall through the window at the Ducor Hotel when the soldiers began shooting her friends. She didn't stand helplessly, calling out their names, watching the pool of blood forming around their bodies soak the sand. Now, they got up after they were shot, and she climbed out of the window using a rope she had made out of sheets, and they all went swimming.

"I'm not going to Liberia. I'm going to Sierra Leone," Catherine said after a minute.

"Didn't your friend say that things were getting bad there too?"

"I don't know what he meant by that, and I don't have time to find out what Heribert was talking about. If there was something I should know, Jules would have told me."

"I don't know, Cat. There's something different about you this year," Justine said. "You're not as jittery. Couldn't going to Africa so close to the anniversary be a mistake? Do you think that's what Madame Chief would want?"

Justine's words weighed heavily on Catherine.

"I can't just sit around waiting anymore. Yes, I'm a little nervous about going to Africa this close to the anniversary, but I'm tired of being controlled by what happened to me in Liberia. Do you know I've never really told anyone what happened to me that night? Not that anyone has ever let me talk about it. I'm figuring things out though, and I've decided that this is the last time the violence that was done to my friends is going to keep me from doing what I need to do. Something keeps pushing me to go to Sierra Leone. I have to go!"

"And what if it all turns out bad? You'll be there all alone. Then what?"

"You can't talk me out of this, Justine," Catherine said. "Africa is my home. It will always be home to me. I was born in America and I like it here, but I don't think of it as home. Someday, I'd like to introduce you to my Africa. TV shows you the violence and poverty of Africa, but Africa is much bigger than that. It's more complex than that. And in my mind, it is the most beautiful place on earth."

"It makes me crazy when you talk like that?" Justine countered. "Do you really know what you're getting into? You haven't been there in over a year. Besides, what can you do there that you can't do from here? You're not going to see Madame Chief on the twelfth and you know it."

"I'll be with her people. Waiting with them makes a difference to me. I don't know what to say to make you understand how hard it is for me to be so far away from her while she's in trouble."

"What about your dad?"

"What about Dad?"

"He's worried about you too."

"I don't know what to tell you, Justine."

"Oh forget it. Your mind is made up, and no one can talk to you," Justine snapped.

Catherine lost patience. "I'm going and that's all there is to it. Accept it or not, right now I don't give a damn."

Hurt, Justine stood up and walked a few feet away. She rocked Sonya, her back to Catherine. Catherine approached her.

"I'm sorry, Justine," she said. "I didn't mean that. It's just all building up inside me. You know I have to go. I won't fall apart, I promise." Tears filled Catherine's eyes. "Nothing's going to happen to me."

Tears streamed down Justine's face as well. "I thought I was supposed to take care of you this time since Mama can't come," she blurted out.

Sonya woke up and stared at them with wide-eyed curiosity. "Mommy," she said, "are you OK? Catty, are you OK?" She placed one little hand on each of their shoulders and patted them both gently.

"Mommy's OK," Justine said and forced a smile. Catherine went into her shoulder bag and pulled out a packet of tissues. She handed one to Justine and took one for herself.

"I'll be all right. I promise you," she reassured Justine. "A woman's got to do what she's got to do. Isn't that what you always say?" Catherine smiled. Justine blew her nose, hugged her tight, and smiled as well.

CHAPTER TEN

April 11
Journey to Freetown

The aroma of hot coffee and warm sweet rolls roused Catherine from sleep. She sat up and checked her watch. A flight attendant brought a tray of warm towels and offered one to her. "It was a long night, wasn't it?" Her voice was sunny.

"Yes, it was," Catherine replied and opened the shutter covering the window next to her seat.

After the flight to Amsterdam, where Catherine intended to stay overnight before taking a plane to Accra, Ghana, and finally a connecting flight to Sierra Leone, the entire trip from New York City to Freetown would take a day and a half, possibly two. She had brought enough clothes for two weeks and $60,000 to buy information and favors and, possibly, to hire mercenaries if necessary. It was all the money her mother had left her.

Most of the money was in large denominations and hidden under the notepaper in a stationery box tucked in the bottom of her satchel. She had small bills in her pockets and wallet. She had decided against traveler's checks. Cash was easier to handle, and on the street, the exchange rate from dollar to leone was greater than at the banks. Those transactions involved no bureaucracy, no hours of waiting while being sent from one clerk to the next.

Catherine had had trouble sleeping because she was nervous, plagued with doubt about her decision, which had no solid justification or support from anyone close to her. Finally, she had imagined Madame Chief saying, "My dear, you are stepping out on faith in coming to rescue me."

As she pondered this, she had drifted off to sleep just as the sun appeared and sat on the wing of the plane. Now she thought about the difficulties she would invariably encounter when she tried to hire mercenaries. *African men,* she thought and sighed.

African men, especially those in the military, where she was sure to find mercenaries, never made deals with women.

I'll have to find an angle or hire a middleman, she mused as she looked out the window.

She ordered coffee and had just enough time to drink it before the plane began its descent.

Schiphol was a modern, busy airport. It was patrolled by Dutch soldiers carrying automatic rifles slung over one shoulder. The customs agents were highly efficient, methodical in their search for illegal items. Conversations with passengers coming into the country were kept to a minimum. The lines moved quickly.

Catherine placed her carry-on bag on the table. An agent with sandy blond hair, casually dressed in a blue shirt, pants, and tie, asked to see her passport.

"How long will you be staying with us?"

"In transit, just overnight."

Catherine watched the agent leaf through her documents. As she looked around the terminal, she suddenly began to feel dizzy and off-balance. Her heart beat rapidly as she strained to find something familiar. In the beginning, this type of panic attack had only happened when the anniversary was close. It had not happened for a long time. Catherine closed her eyes and fought to control her breathing.

"Are you all right, madame?" the agent asked, looking concerned.

"I'll be fine," Catherine replied, her balance slowly coming back.

Outside, she hailed a taxi and went to the Sofitel Hotel. She requested the room she had stayed in the last time she was there.

The room was small, with high ceilings and floral wallpaper. The bed had been turned back, showing the fine-quality sheets. Catherine sat on the edge. She felt shaky and tired. She called Marcus and felt better after talking to him. Then she called Jules, not trusting that he would keep her apprised of developments concerning Madame Chief even though he had said he would.

"Hello. This is the Coleman residence."

"Mendee, it's Ms. Catherine calling."

"Oh," the maid said excitedly, "Ms. Catherine. It is so nice to hear your voice."

"How de body?" Catherine said.

"De body's fine. And you, Ms. Catherine?"

"De body's fine," Catherine replied. "May I speak to Mr. Coleman?"

"He went upcountry very early this morning."

"Did he say what time he was coming back?" Catherine inquired, surprised.

"No, Ms. Catherine, but I think it will be late."

"Is Madam Celeste at home?"

"Sorry, Ms. Catherine. Ms. Celeste and the cook went to the market."

"Please, tell her I called."

"I will as soon as she comes home."

Catherine thanked the maid and hung up.

Jules had told her that he had to pick up two advisors from the UN that morning.

What's going on, Jules? You can't be in two places at once. I should call the embassy. Suddenly she felt dog tired. *Maybe later,* she thought and began undressing. Her arms felt like two weights. She turned on the television to a children's program and drifted off.

Three hours later, Catherine sat up. After a moment of disorientation passed, she decided to call her friend Hans Mendelssohn.

A childhood friend, Hans had attended the International School in Liberia when Catherine was there. He had a habit of popping in and out of her life, but she had not seen him for a while. He had called the day after she booked the flight to Sierra Leone.

Hans was excited to see her. He squeezed her tightly with his skinny long arms and looked at her intently for a moment. "How have you been?" Catherine asked.

"I'm making it," he replied.

Though thin, he had gained a little weight since the last time Catherine had seen him, and he was wearing a ponytail. She was the first person he had seen from the International School in two years. Only a few people knew where he was. He had developed a heroin addiction while traveling in Asia and was living in a residence with other former addicts. He had been through three rehabs and was clean for over a year.

"And you? Is everything all right?"

"I'm fine."

She wondered what he had heard. He was in Switzerland attending a wedding when the coup took place. His family had not come back to Liberia after that. He had also lost friends that night.

They ate dinner at the hotel, went for a walk, and talked about old times. Hans did imitations of all their teachers. Catherine laughed until a cramp grabbed her side. For a moment, she forgot why she was in Amsterdam.

She kissed his cheek when he brought her back to the hotel and asked him to come to Philadelphia next time he visited the States.

"Don't make me have to come looking for you, Hans."

A strange look came on his face. Then he laughed and promised to put her name at the top of his list. She did not count on seeing him again anytime soon. She knew him that well.

Later that evening, she called him when she could not get to sleep. They talked until three in the morning.

April 12

Catherine overslept. She slept through the hour that she and Madame Chief would have awakened to go to the gravesite and complete the ritual. She had not had to face those hours alone. *Thank you, Lord, for grace,* she whispered. She sat on the floor, closed her eyes, and remembered each of her friends. It was good to be with them again. Afterward, she imagined casting the seeds over the grave and Madame Chief smiling.

As usual, the traffic to the airport was congested. The taxi driver watched her warily in the rearview mirror. Catherine wondered what showed on her face. An airplane passed overhead coming in for a landing. Catherine watched it for a moment and closed her eyes. She took a deep breath. *I'll be OK as soon as I reach Sierra Leone.*

On the way to the gate, she stopped in a gift shop and bought a bag of nuts in the likely event that the ferry from Lungi Island, where Freetown's airport was located, to Freetown was delayed. She could not afford to eat the food being cooked on the docks. Too much time had passed since she had eaten the fruits and fresh fish that were found in the open markets. She worried a little about how her stomach would hold up when the tiny microbes that usually made foreigners develop diarrhea found their way into her stomach. She decided that when it happened, she would not complain like a foreigner.

The plane to Ghana glided in the heavens with the help of a strong tailwind and touched down just as smoothly.

When the door opened, passengers walked across the tarmac to the terminal. The surface was as hot as an oven. A blast of African heat hit Catherine square in the face when she stepped through the door of the plane. The air was thick and humid, making breathing incredibly difficult. Fortunately, a light blue and white KLM airplane connecting Accra, Ghana, to Freetown, Sierra Leone, was already waiting at the gate.

It was a full flight. Half of the passengers were market women. The rest were nongovernmental workers (NGOs) who worked in development. There were also diplomats, a few Europeans on vacation, and businessmen dressed in political suits, or suits and ties. As usual, Catherine had a window seat.

An African in a political suit made his way up the aisle and stopped at her seat. He opened the compartment above her head and moved things around, then shoved his briefcase and a package wrapped in white paper inside. She avoided his gaze by keeping her nose in a magazine. Before sitting down, he turned to see who else was on the plane. When he sat down, he scrutinized everyone who came on board.

"Oh, excuse me," he said after accidentally bumping her arm while fidgeting with his seat belt. He had a British accent.

"That's all right," said Catherine. She glanced at him, smiled politely, and went back to reading.

"My name is Richard Acolatse," he said.

She put the magazine down slowly and looked at him. He smiled, trying to charm her. She guessed that they were about the same age.

"It's nice to meet you, Richard. I'm Catherine."

"Ah. An American who has lived in England?"

"Excuse me?"

"I detect a bit of a British accent," Richard said and flashed a smile.

"Oh," Catherine said casually and looked out the window.

"I went to a British boarding school," Richard continued.

"Which one?" Catherine turned back toward him, her curiosity piqued.

"So you are familiar with England?" Richard chuckled.

"Yes, but I'm an American."

"New York is my favorite city in the United States. Do you live in New York?"

"No, I'm from Philadelphia."

"I've visited Philadelphia," Richard said and launched into a story about the City of Brotherly Love and Sisterly Affection, a vernacular he seemed to find amusing. He then went on to tell her about the last time he was in New York, his visit to Vermont, a planned trip to Paris, and his friends in London. Catherine quickly tired of his conversation.

"Excuse me," said Catherine.

She stood up and brushed by Richard as he stepped into the aisle. She went to the restroom, splashed water on her face, and came out. While standing in the back of the plane, it occurred to her that after twenty minutes of listening to Richard prattle on, she still didn't know what he did for a living. *He's probably a diamond smuggler,* she thought. Richard had mentioned that he was coming from Antwerp, Belgium, the diamond capital of the world. Catherine found it quite easy to picture him in a back room in Belgium, arguing with a jeweler over the price of a diamond.

He probably works with De Beers. I wonder how much they gave him for his blood diamonds. Those damn diamonds fund coups and rebels, and the rebels have Mama. Her face became hot with anger.

The signal that the plane was about to descend came on.

"I suppose someone is meeting you, Ms. Catherine?" Richard questioned when Catherine finally returned to her seat.

"Yes," Catherine lied without looking at him.

"Well, I hope you have a very nice time in Sierra Leone."

"Thank you," she replied. Turning to Richard and looking him directly in the eye, she added, "Tell me, Richard, what business are you in?"

Richard hesitated. "I'm in the exporting business."

"What exactly do you export?"

"Just about anything that can be exported, mostly minerals."

"Do you work for a company, or are you an independent?"

"Both. My family has a business," Richard answered casually.

The plane landed on Lungi Island and taxied toward the terminal. As it slowed down, some of the passengers stood up and pulled items out of the overhead compartments. Richard and Catherine waited until the plane came to a full stop. Richard continued talking. Catherine watched the ground crew.

"Well, it was nice meeting you, Ms. Lloyd," Richard said, drawing Catherine's attention back to him.

"And you," Catherine said.

As Richard stood up and opened the overheard compartment, Catherine looked at him closely and thought that he reminded her of a certain paramount chief who had twenty children, a number of whom had been raised abroad. "Your grandfather wouldn't happen to be Ebenezer Jusufu, would he?" Catherine asked. Richard's expression went blank, and the smile melted off his face. His demeanor cooled. He sat his briefcase on the arm of the seat and stared directly at Catherine. Then, his lips twisted into a smirk.

"If you will have dinner with me while you are in Freetown, I might tell you about my family tree."

"That's nice of you to offer," Catherine said coolly, "but I'm not staying long. Thank you for the invitation."

Catherine was the last person to get off the plane. She had sat for a moment, wondering, *How did he know my last name?* She was sure she had not told him.

"Please have your passports available for inspection. The queues for customs are over there."

An airport official dressed in uniform pointed in the direction of three tables with signs taped to the front: Nationals, ECOWAS Members, and Non–Sierra Leone Citizens. Catherine got in line with other noncitizens. Each table had three officials waiting to check passports.

When she reached the front of the line, Catherine handed her passport to one of the officials.

"How long are you going to be here?" he asked without looking at her. He turned the page to her photo ID.

"My plans are not definite," Catherine replied.

The official's eyes widened when he saw Catherine's picture. He looked up. "Ms. Catherine?" he said, standing and grinning from ear to ear.

"Ibrahim!" Catherine instantly recognized the young man and was delighted to see him. Ibrahim's mother had cooked for Catherine when she was a child. "It is so good to see you." She reached out, took his hands in hers, and smiled warmly.

"How are you, Ms. Catherine? It's nice to see you again."

"I am well. How long have you been working here?"

"Over a year, Ms. Catherine."

"Your mother, how is she?"

"She is fine. She is getting older though and having trouble getting around. I will tell her you asked." The more they talked, the brighter Ibrahim's smile became.

"Please tell your mother I will stop by to see her."

"Yes, of course." His expression then sobered. "You have heard about Mama, I suppose."

"Yes. That is why I am here."

Ibrahim nodded. He stamped Catherine's visa and handed the passport back to her. She slipped her hand into her pocket and palmed a $10 bill.

"Welcome home, Ms. Catherine," Ibrahim said. Catherine took his hand in hers and passed the bill to him. He eased it into his pocket and nodded his appreciation.

"Thank you, Ibrahim."

Baggage from the plane was placed in a six-by-ten-by-four-foot window. The crew had stacked it high by the time Catherine went over to look for her suitcase. It wasn't there. The truck left and came back three more times with baggage. Other passengers retrieved their suitcases, and the crowd thinned. Forty minutes passed and still no suitcase. She found a soda vending machine and bought a Coca-Cola. Exhausted, she drank the soda and hoped for a caffeine rush. *I wonder if my baggage made the connections,* she thought but was not troubled by the idea. She had lost baggage before. The day she left the States, she had checked to see if the ferries were working. They were working, but they often broke down and the wait could be several hours. Jules had told her that he would try to send someone to meet her on Lungi Island, but she wondered if he had had the time to arrange it, given his unscheduled trip to the refugee camp.

She looked around for a place to sit. The benches in the terminal were crowded with people. Wearily, she looked at the baggage handlers hoisting unclaimed baggage out of the window and wondered if one of them could tell her if there was any luggage left on the plane.

An old man bent over the suitcases, diligently organizing the pieces, pushing them together in neat rows, caught her attention. Catherine walked over to him. "Excuse me," she said. "Do you know if the truck is coming back with more baggage?" He looked up at her and blinked. She wasn't sure if he understood what she was saying, so she switched to Mende. He smiled, nodded vehemently, and told her more was on the way.

A minute later, the truck came back with her suitcase.

In countries where there is a shortage of specialty items for women, female customs agents had a reputation of being thorough, especially when examining the suitcases belonging to other women. A female customs agent was on duty today, and an alarm went off in Catherine's head. She immediately came alert. Her elbow clamped down on her satchel as she thought about the woman going through the purse and discovering the money.

The agent was a large-boned woman in her thirties. She wore a plain African-style dress. She motioned for Catherine to open her suitcase. Her eyes grew greedy as she looked inside.

She lifted Catherine's jeans, skirts, dresses, shoes, teddy pajamas, robe, designer bras, and panties up in the air. She examined them, front and back. She opened the tubes of lipstick and the makeup case and peered into the mirror. She opened bottles of lotion and sniffed them. As she carelessly went through the carry-on, some of Catherine's things fell on the floor. Catherine bristled. *Stay calm,* she told herself. Satisfaction was written all over the agent's face until she spotted the satchel. She pushed the carry-on to one side, cleared a space for the handbag, and pointed.

"Come, come now. I must go tru dat too," she said, scowling and waving her hand.

Catherine did not move.

"If you don't mind, I would like to take everything out of my purse and put it on the table for you," Catherine said in Mende. She took the satchel off her shoulder and opened the drawstring.

The agent was thrown by hearing a foreigner speak a tribal language, but that lasted only a moment. "No, I will go through it myself," she insisted in Mende. She leaned over the table and grabbed the satchel.

Catherine glowered and snatched it back.

There were two male agents standing nearby. They quickly pulled the female agent aside and spoke to her in Mende. The woman shook her head in adamant refusal as they tried to convince her to let Catherine go. Catherine squared her shoulders, ready to hold off anyone who tried to go through the satchel. Suddenly everyone stopped talking and looked beyond her. Catherine turned and saw Ibrahim. His eyes were locked onto the woman. "You go now. Go, go," she said nervously and waved Catherine on.

At the exit, an official asked to see Catherine's passport. He did not have a uniform, but a badge was pinned to the front of his shirt. Mechanically, Catherine gave it to him. Her hand shook from the adrenaline still surging in her body from the encounter with the female agent. This final check was new. Catherine concluded that there was no real purpose for it other than to help the man support his family. "Welcome to Sierra Leone," he said pleasantly.

The familiar blare of car horns greeted Catherine when she came out of the terminal. The night air was warm and humid. Taxis with passengers crowded in the front and backseats were bottlenecked on the road leading out of the airport. She looked up at the stars and the blue-black velvet sky and found a second wind. A lovely childhood memory came to her of lying in bed, gazing up at the moon and stars through an open window. She had imagined then what it might be like to float up into the cosmos, to the Milky Way. The memory was soothing.

"Ms. Catherine?" A man was coming toward her. The light was too dim to make out his face. He stepped into the light.

"Benjamin?" Catherine said, stunned.

"Yes, Ms. Catherine," Benjamin rejoined. "It's me."

"Benjamin," Catherine stammered. He smiled. Her eyes brushed over his graying hair, the age lines around his kind eyes, his strong hands, and the plain shirt and pants he wore.

Benjamin stepped up to Catherine. She leaned toward him and kissed him on both cheeks.

"What are you doing here?" she asked as if he had stepped into one of her dreams.

"I came for you, Ms. Catherine. It is all over the village. Mr. Coleman said it would be all right."

Yes, of course. God bless you, Jules.

She wanted to hold Benjamin's hands and dance joyfully.

"How long have you been waiting?" she asked, not knowing what to say to a man she'd assumed dead.

"Not long," Benjamin replied. "Let me help you with these."

Benjamin found a cart and put Catherine's suitcases on it.

She felt overwhelmed. *Kismet. It has to be. The ancestors are telling me I should be here.*

On starry nights, locals sat on their porches, watching the stream of cars passing by on the road to the ferry. If it had been daytime, Catherine would have waved at them, and they would have waved back. Some of the houses were built out of stone with tar roofs. Others had concrete walls and thatched roofs. Every house had a porch. There were candles sitting on the rails of the houses without electricity. Larger houses had electric generators. The rooms inside these houses were bathed in yellow light. Catherine fought to keep her eyes open. She wanted to ask Benjamin about Mama. She wanted verification of what she had heard. But exhaustion exacted its due, and within minutes, she fell deeply asleep.

Catherine woke up and looked into a pitch blackness punctuated only by candles and the fires in metal drums that lit the docking area. The moon was full. Benjamin was standing outside the car.

"What time is it, Benjamin?" Catherine asked, looking around to get her bearings.

"It is midnight," Benjamin replied. He opened the car door, and Catherine got out.

"Did we miss the ferry?"

"Unfortunately yes. But the ferry man say the ferries had been working fine all day. One will be along soon."

The dock was busy. The light of the full moon made it easy for the locals to conduct their affairs. They milled around and stopped to greet one another. They spoke in low voices, their bodies outlined by the blazing fires of the metal drums. The vendors sold bananas, mangos, papaya, palm and coconut oil, and fish. Discarded peels from the fruit littered the ground. Hunger rumbled in Catherine's empty stomach. She thought about the nuts in her purse, but she had no appetite for them. She wanted the food on the dock.

"I think I will buy a banana," she said to Benjamin and approached a vendor.

After selecting a bunch of bananas, Catherine handed the woman a dollar. The market woman unraveled the bulging fold of material tied at her waist, where she kept her money, and handed Catherine ninety leone in change. Catherine was stunned by the exchange rate. It was twice what she thought it would be. She divided the bills, put one half in her pocket, handed the other half back to the market woman, and walked away.

"Walk with me, Benjamin," Catherine said and started up the dock to a spot she had claimed many years ago. As they started out, Benjamin walked several paces behind her. When Catherine turned to him and said, "Walk beside me, please," he did.

They found the place. Benjamin searched for a clean piece of paper for Catherine to sit on. She positioned it where she normally sat and looked out at the blue-black water, shimmering in the moonlight, for a long time before speaking.

"How are you really, Benjamin?"

"I am well, Ms. Catherine," Benjamin said reassuringly.

Catherine hesitated. "Would you please tell me what happened?"

Benjamin looked puzzled. "You don't know?" It was inconceivable to him that Catherine would be uninformed about Mama in any way.

"People have told me a lot of things, but you were there. You saw everything."

"I will do my best, Ms. Catherine."

He told her everything that had happened, starting with the day David Banyo came to Madame Chief's house. He believed that was where it all started because Madame Chief would not have been kidnapped if she had not decided to go to Freetown that day. She'd had plans to visit her uncle.

"The petrol it finished and the car died, so we carried Mama for miles one time," Benjamin said as he continued to tell the story. "Mama talked to them every day about something or another thing about Liberia. A truck came up pretty soon. They got in and took Mama with them. I did not want to leave her. It hurt my heart so bad. But she told me to go home and tell what I heard and seen so that no one would be sick about this thing that happened to her."

"I am sick about this thing. How dare they take her, Benjamin?" Catherine said angrily.

"These boys are afraid to hurt Mama," Benjamin said. "They will be careful with her."

"How do you know that? What makes you so sure?"

"She is a female paramount chief!"

Something in his pronouncement made Catherine feel foolish. "Benjamin, what am I doing here?" she whispered.

"You heard the drum calling you to come back to Sierra Leone," Benjamin said with gentle assurance. "So you have come here to be with us, to wait with us until Mama comes home. It is a good place to be. There is no place better."

The ferry boat bell clanked.

"We should go now. There is no need to hurry though," Benjamin said. They stood up. He brushed the dirt off his pants.

"The ship's bell is actually working?" Catherine said as they began walking.

"For now. It will break again soon," Benjamin said. "You know. Nothing mechanical works for long in Sierra Leone."

CHAPTER ELEVEN

April 13
Freetown

A persistent knock on the door broke through her pink-and-blue dream of a carnival on a white sandy beach. Catherine opened one eye.

"Catherine, it's me, Celeste."

"Just a minute," Catherine said, rolling out of bed and scooping up her robe from a crumbled heap of clothes on the floor.

"I thought you might want this," Celeste said, holding a cup of black coffee to Catherine's nose when she opened the door. They touched cheeks. "Thanks, Celeste," Catherine said, closing the door behind her.

Jules's wife was noticeably pregnant. She wore a tent-like green and white African print top, matching pants, and white sandals. Her face was fuller than the last time Catherine had seen her—a year ago at her wedding—but everything else about her was just the same: dazzling smile, perfect white teeth, almond shaped eyes, clear dark reddish brown skin. Her voice was like that of a singer, clear as a bell. She was almost as tall as Catherine, but she hunched a bit when she walked. Her hair was cut short in an Afro.

Once when Catherine had asked Jules how Celeste was adjusting to Sierra Leone and Freetown, he had said that Celeste hardly ever stayed home, that in three months, she knew everyone in Freetown and could barely move more than a few feet without someone stopping to talk to her.

Celeste stood in the middle of the floor and looked around at the comfortable furniture and queen-size bed. "It feels nice in here," she said, commenting on the air-conditioned room.

"Please make yourself at home," Catherine said, motioning to a table and chair near the door that leads to a sundeck. Catherine followed her to the table, and she opened the curtains covering the door. Bright light spilled into the room.

The Hotel Bintumani sat at the top of a mountain, overlooking a spectacular view of rolling hills and cliffs. At night, the city below sparkled with lights shining out the windows of Freetown houses. As Catherine looked out at the lush tropical garden filled with exotic flowers, palm trees, vines and broad-leaf plants surrounding the hotel, and beyond it Lumley Beach and the Great South Atlantic Ocean, she felt herself reviving from the long journey.

There were several fine hotels in Freetown, but the Bintumani was the only four-star property. Sierra Leone's upper class, wealthy businessmen, entrepreneurs, and foreigners preferred it. The lobby featured a massive dark teak floor-to-ceiling carving with the hotel's name carved into it. It befitted the hotel's grandness.

Catherine loved the Bintumani, but this time she chose it for one reason only: sooner or later everyone found their way to the Bintumani, and they carried information and secrets that were for sale.

Catherine eased down in the seat opposite Celeste, who had been watching her intently.

"The ferry didn't come until one thirty this morning," Catherine said, making light conversation.

She didn't know Celeste well. Aside from a few receptions and cookouts that Jules had brought Celeste to, the longest period Catherine had spent with Celeste was on a train ride from Philadelphia to Washington when a spur-of-the-moment trip to Washington had placed her on the same train Celeste was traveling on from New York to DC.

"Hope I didn't wake you too early," Celeste said apologetically.

"No, not at all. What time is it anyway?"

"It's one o'clock."

That late already? "Where's Jules?" Catherine asked.

"At work."

So he did get back.

"He's going to be tied up in meetings all day, so he asked me to check on you, to see if there's anything you need."

He must have pushed hard to do everything in one day. What was he doing upcountry anyway?

"Can I offer you something?" Catherine asked and smiled pleasantly at Celeste.

"No, thank you. I'm fine," Celeste replied.

They lapsed into silence. Celeste looked around the room again. "I've always liked the rooms in this hotel," she commented.

"Me too," Catherine responded. "Did Jules tell you I drink black coffee?"

"No, I just forgot to bring cream along. I take my coffee black, and so does Jules."

"Well now, that must make us kin or something," Catherine joked.

Celeste looked at her blankly. The awkward moment passed. "So how long were you planning to stay at the Bintumani?" Celeste said finally. "We would love to have you come stay with us for a few days, or as long as you like."

"Let me think about it. I'll let you know," Catherine replied. She didn't want Jules looking over her shoulder. She hoped Celeste did not feel put off by the less-than-enthusiastic response to her invitation.

"Whenever you're ready," Celeste said. She lightly drummed her fingers on the table. "Well, I guess I'll be going now. We would like to have you over for dinner tonight if you're not busy." She stood up.

"Busy day?" Catherine asked, looking up but not moving.

"Not really."

"Well, how about hanging out with me? I could use the company."

Celeste flashed a brilliant smile and sat back down.

"Great! I'll go take a quick shower." Catherine strolled over to her suitcase. "I packed this month's *Essence* and *The New Yorker*," she said, searching the outer pockets.

The expression on Celeste's face when Catherine handed her the magazine was priceless. Her eyes fixed on a picture of the confident-looking smartly dressed, attractive black woman on the cover. "I would have given my right arm for a copy of this month's *Essence*," she said. "*The New Yorker* too? I haven't seen *The New Yorker* since the last time I was home."

Home for Celeste was Cleveland, Ohio. She had been living in Washington, DC, working for the USAID Africa Bureau when she met Jules.

Catherine showered and dressed in a half hour. They stopped at the front desk, and Catherine left a message for Marcus in case he called. She also ordered four bottles of water and asked the clerk to have them put in her room. On the way out, she picked up one more.

Celeste's driver, Lansana, was in his late twenties. He leaned against the car with his arms crossed. His white shirt and blue pants were freshly pressed.

"Lansana, this is Ms. Catherine," Celeste said as he opened the door of the olive green Peugeot Roadmaster.

"Good morning, Ms. Catherine." Like most people from Sierra Leone, his smile was warm and welcoming and somewhat infectious.

"Good morning, Lansana," Catherine said.

"Where would you like to go first?" Celeste asked when they settled in the backseat of the car.

"How about the Paramount Hotel?"

Lansana, whose ear was turned toward them, nodded.

The road to Freetown circled down the mountain. Catherine rolled down the window. They rounded a curve dangerously close to the edge of the road and a drop straight down hundreds of feet. "Whew!" Catherine pulled back.

"I have the same reaction when I'm sitting on that side of the car," Celeste remarked.

At the bottom of the hill, the traffic came to a dead halt. Mercedes Benzes, scooters, buses, old rusting junkers, Toyota trucks, and bicycles all lined up as a farmer drove a herd of goats across the road. During midday, the single road into downtown was always gridlocked.

On the side of the road, vendors sold bush meat, fish three and four feet in length, cassava leaves, and other produce. Everyone bought something. There were groups of three, four, and five children moving from car to car, peering into the backseats. They held out their small hands, hopeful that a benefactor would pass a leone or two out the window. Catherine handed leones to them indiscriminately. She spoke playfully to them in Krio. Their laughter sprang into the air. "Thank you, thank you," they said and walked away, sometimes counting, sometimes comparing their gifts. Soon she was out of money. She was satisfied. She went into her purse and pulled out twenty dollars. Celeste stole a curious look at her.

"Lansana, could you exchange this for me when we get in town?" Catherine asked, handing the money over his shoulder. He put it in the glove compartment.

Traffic moved a few kilometers then came to a sudden halt as the car in front of them bumped into the car ahead of it. The man in the front car leaned out of the window and yelled in Krio to the other driver. He waved his hand and laughed, showing all of his white teeth. Catherine reflected on the many times she had seen this kind of laid-back reaction to minor accidents. Then she noticed two men standing at a gas pump, arguing over fuel. This surprised her.

"What's the gas situation in Freetown?" she asked Celeste.

"Awful. The tankers haven't been here in almost two months, and the pumps around town are going dry," Celeste reported.

Catherine glanced at the fuel gauge in the Peugeot. The needle indicated that the gas tank was full. "I see the embassy is doing OK."

"For now but . . ." Celeste made a face.

Catherine waited in vain for Celeste to finish her sentence. She had heard that there was a fuel shortage but not the extent of it. The traffic began moving again. She looked out the window and noticed garbage piled up.

"Mama mentioned something about people buying up electrical generators, but she didn't seem concerned about it."

"How long ago was that?" Celeste said, turning to her.

"Around the beginning of the year," Catherine said.

"Things weren't quite as bad then," Celeste replied. "Did Madame Chief mention that the level of security forces has increased around the city? Foday favors them. He keeps them around to do his dirt. They try to hide in plain clothes, but if you know what to look for, you can easily spot them."

"She never mentioned that." Catherine was puzzled.

"I think they've become more threatening in the past two weeks. They want more dash, and they're pushing people around when they don't get it. They haven't been paid in several months . . ." Celeste took a furtive glance at Lansana. She leaned toward Catherine and whispered, "People are disappearing. His brother . . ." Celeste nodded in Lansana's direction.

Lansana glanced at her through the rearview mirror. Celeste straightened up.

"But the beer is still flowing," she added cynically.

They came to the government buildings in the downtown area. Catherine spotted the Cotton Tree, a national landmark. She was as awed as ever by the old tree. Her eyes followed the branches up to the sky. She was tempted to ask Lansana to stop the car so that she could get out and touch it, stand close to it and feel its ancient aura, its timelessness, its permanence in spite of the changing world around it. They continued past the old oak to the Paramount Hotel. She did not know what she expected to find there. But it was the best place to make contacts.

The Paramount Hotel was one of two downtown hotels frequented by the locals, senior government officials, members of the diplomatic corps, NGO workers, businessmen, and entrepreneurs. It was their preferred watering hole. Foreign-service workers who regularly visited Sierra Leone also went to the Paramount. The hotel needed a fresh coat of paint, but that had been the case as far back as Catherine could remember. Otherwise, it was maintained well enough.

The front lobby was a small room with a few tables and chairs. The registration desk was to the right, and elevators were to the left. Lunch and dinner was served in the second lobby. Catherine and Celeste decided to go there to lunch and wait.

The second lobby smelled of the food cooking in the kitchen. They took a seat at a table. Catherine sat facing the door. Off to the side of the second lobby was a staircase topped by a sign that read Steven's Bar and Grill. An arrow pointed down the steps to the lower level of the hotel.

A waiter came to the table.

"I'll have a cup of espresso," Catherine said.

"Coke for me," said Celeste.

"How's the Jolof rice here these days?" Catherine asked.

"Very good," Celeste replied.

Thoughts about her stomach reacting badly to her favorite African meal popped into Catherine's head as they both ordered the rice. She pushed them aside and thought about the savory flavor of Jolof rice as her empty stomach growled.

A man in an African suit came into the eating area. He waved to Celeste and headed down the stairs.

"So when was the last time you were in the States?" Catherine asked.

"About five months ago," said Celeste. "My great-grandmother turned ninety, and the family gave her a party."

"Do you come from a big family?"

"Pretty big. How about you?"

"Oh, there are quite a few of us. How do you like Africa?"

"I love it," Celeste responded brightly. "I feel blessed to have met Jules and to be living here. It's such an opportunity to be able to do more hands-on work on the AIDS problem."

The waiter came back with the espresso in a demicup and a piece of lemon on the saucer and a coke in a tall glass.

"Jules told me you attended Georgetown," Catherine said.

"I was in graduate school the same year you came in as an undergraduate," Celeste replied.

"Well, now I know we're related," Catherine joked.

Celeste smiled.

"I'll be glad when Madame Chief comes home," Celeste said, suddenly pensive. "She offered to help by endorsing the information center for women we're trying to start up. She had some ideas about how to bring the men in too. She's very worried about how quickly HIV is spreading through the villages."

"I know," Catherine said and thought about how Celeste had referred to Madame Chief's absence as if Mama was away on one of her missions and in no trouble at all. Perplexed, she concluded that Celeste had not been in Africa long enough to understand the impact Mama's abduction was having on her people.

A man came in the room and said something to their waiter.

"Do you know him?" Catherine asked. Something about him had caught the corner of her eye. He was dressed like a businessman, but he needed a haircut and his shoes were old.

"He's one of Fofana's flunkies. He's not even from around here."

Catherine was glad her back wasn't to the door. They watched him until he left.

"Before I left USAID, we were trying to figure out how AIDS was traveling so quickly from one African country to the next," Celeste said. "I think we're on to it now. We were spending so much time interviewing the women with HIV about their sexual habits that we missed it. Now some of us think it's being spread by the soldiers. A couple of my colleagues think the truckers are the main source."

The waiter came back with their lunch. Catherine tasted the rice. *Justine would love this. I wonder if Clifton would too.* She sighed and ate her first full meal in days.

The clock on the wall read four-thirty. A group of four men, Africans dressed in tailored political suits, went down to the bar. A minute later, a Caucasian man came in and went down the stairs.

"It looks like quitting time," said Catherine.

They finished eating, paid the check, and headed for Steven's Bar and Grill.

The grill was a no-frills establishment. On one side of the room, there was a large bar. The floors were wood, and bare wooden tables and chairs were in the center of the room. The only picture hanging on the wall was one of President Foday Payne dressed in a uniform covered with insignias. Catherine and Celeste found a seat and ordered water.

A group of peace corps workers in their early twenties—three Caucasians, two Asians, and two African Americans—took the table next to Catherine and Celeste. The two African Americans made eye contact with Catherine and nodded. A white woman wearing traditional dress, her long brown hair pulled back in a ponytail, came in with an African wearing a suit and tie. They took a seat at the bar. "I haven't seen them in ages," Catherine said, nodding in their direction.

Celeste turned. "George and Sanghor? They went back to the States for a little while. I think they have about four children now."

"I see Malcolm Chamberlain is back," Catherine remarked as an African American man came in the bar.

"That brother will go to his grave wearing his cap turned backwards," Celeste said with a smile.

Malcolm was in his early forties. He had worked for Jules's father as his economics officer. He spotted Celeste and walked toward the table carrying his drink. When he saw Catherine, he stopped in his tracks and broke out in a smile.

"Well I'll be damned! Catherine Lloyd." Malcolm leaned over and kissed her on both cheeks. "When did you get back?" he asked, pulling out a chair and sitting down.

"I arrived yesterday," Catherine replied.

"I heard you were coming through. It's so good to see you, girl." He tapped Catherine affectionately on the arm. Malcolm's smile was so large it seemed to take up most of his face.

"I hear you went native," said Catherine, referring to the practice of a foreigner marrying an African woman.

"One day back in Freetown, and you're right back into it," Malcolm chuckled. "You probably know my wife. Her name was Sonia Gbomba. Do you remember her?"

"Oh yes, I know her."

"I bought a chicken farm too."

"Now, Malcolm, what are you doing with a chicken farm?" Catherine teased. "You're a city boy. I bet your wife is the real farmer."

"I'm originally from Greensboro, North Carolina. I grew up around chickens."

"Really?"

"Sho nuf," Malcolm replied. His eyes twinkled.

"Malcolm, you're making this all up. Where's your accent?"

"I dropped it somewhere between the Mason-Dixon Line and New York. I swear," he said, holding up two fingers like a Boy Scout. "Ask my friend over there."

He turned and waved to a man dressed in a pair of slacks and an open-collar shirt sitting at the bar. The man picked up his beer and came toward them.

"Hi, Kwasi," Celeste said.

"Hello, Madame Celeste."

"Catherine, this is my partner, Kwasi. Kwasi, Catherine. Kwasi's from Ghana."

"It's very nice to meet you, Ms. Catherine." Kwasi had a quiet voice, the exact opposite of Malcolm.

"It's nice to meet you," Catherine said. "Please sit down."

"So you and Malcolm are in business together," Catherine said, smiling. "Malcolm was just singing your praises. He was telling us about how quickly you learned chicken farming from him. Isn't that right, Malcolm?"

Kwasi smiled politely and glanced at Malcolm.

"OK, Ms. Catherine," Malcolm said. "My friend Kwasi approached me with this idea for a business before I left to go work at our embassy in Guinea." He placed his large smooth hand on Kwasi's shoulder. "He's the real mastermind. I get the clients and manage the business, and he takes care of the chickens. We're going to expand to cattle later this year. Right, Kwasi?"

Kwasi smiled.

"So what does your father really do for a living?"

"He's a dentist. I grew up in Chicago," Malcolm said sheepishly.

Catherine laughed. "You should be ashamed of yourself, Malcolm."

Friendly banter soon gave way to a sobering discussion about the political situation in Sierra Leone. Catherine listened quietly, watching to see who came into the bar.

"Something has to be done soon. Civil servants haven't been paid in months, and the price of rice is so high people can barely afford it. The women are particularly angry about that," Celeste exclaimed.

"Did you hear that a group of men from Madame Chief's village tried to cross the border into Liberia yesterday?" Malcolm commented.

"What happened?" Catherine asked.

"Foday sent soldiers after them and brought them back," Malcolm said with a frown. "The people in her village are beside themselves."

"For Pete's sake, why didn't he just let them go?" Catherine wondered, frustration in her voice. Everyone became silent.

Malcolm leaned into Catherine. "You know this thing is about to blow." Malcolm attempted to whisper, but his voice carried, and one of the peace corps workers turned and looked at him.

"What do you mean?" Catherine asked, fearful that it was the same something Heribert had talked about.

Suddenly Malcolm looked beyond her, and his face clouded with anger. They turned to see whom he was staring at. Richard Acolatse, the man Catherine had met on the plane from Ghana, was standing in the door, scanning the room. He spotted Catherine and made his way to the table.

"What does that mother fu—," Malcolm stopped himself. "Excuse me, ladies," he apologized.

"Ms. Catherine, it's so nice to see you again. I see you have found the Parliament," Richard said when he reached them.

"Does everyone know Richard Acolatse? We met on the plane from Ghana," Catherine said. His gaze felt slimy. Catherine looked around the table to gauge how the others were reacting.

"Hello, Richard," Celeste said coolly.

Malcolm turned away from Richard and took a long deliberate swig from his bottle of beer. Richard glanced at him. "Ms. Celeste," he said, "it's always a pleasure to see you."

"Kwasi, I'll be in my office early tomorrow if you'd like to give me a call," Richard added.

Kwasi stole a furtive glance at Malcolm.

"Well, it was nice running into you, Ms. Catherine. I hope to see you again some time." He eased away from the table.

How did he know my last name? Catherine felt her skin crawl.

"Where are you staying?" Malcolm asked Catherine.

"The Bintumani. Why?" She sensed something behind Malcolm's question.

"Let me give you a tip. Stay away from Richard Acolatse. He's bad news."

"Is Richard involved in diamond smuggling?"

"Yes," Malcolm said with derision, "but he's just a delivery boy."

"That figures."

"His father treats him like some sort of pimp."

Catherine looked over at Richard. He nodded at her and left the bar.

"I can deal with Richard. Right, Kwasi?" Malcolm eyed Kwasi. Kwasi squirmed. "But you should steer clear of him, Catherine. I've heard he's trying to get something going on the side. You don't want to keep company with someone like Richard."

"Don't start rumors, Malcolm," cautioned Celeste.

"He's getting into the guns," said Malcolm, ignoring Celeste's warning. "He'll take anything for them that the Liberian rebels he's doing business with can get their hands on. It's a damn shame. Liberia will never get on its feet with people like him around."

Malcolm pulled out a business card from his wallet. "If you need anything, give me a call," he said, handing it to Catherine. He stood up, and Kwasi followed suit. "It was nice meeting you, Ms. Catherine." Kwasi bowed slightly from the waist, and then they were gone.

"Had enough for one day?" Celeste asked.

"Not quite," Catherine said.

"You look a little tired."

"I'm fine. What time is dinner?"

"Seven o'clock." Celeste nodded at a man and woman who had just come through the door. "Excuse me, someone I need to talk to just walked in."

Catherine continued to keep watch on the door. The bar filled as more people arrived.

Catherine noticed how Celeste became animated while talking to the couple. They nodded in agreement. Catherine wondered what was making her so intense.

I guess I should call it a day, Catherine mused, feeling her energy drain. Just then, Henry Koroma, President Foday Payne's chief advisor, and Dr. Amadu Mensa entered the bar.

Henry Koroma had round cheeks, a booming voice, and an effusive nature. He reminded Catherine of a black Santa Claus. His hair was completely white. He was what she called a survivalist, a man who lands on his feet no matter what the political climate. Dr. Mensa towered over Henry. Catherine had not seen him since he received his degree from Oxford and began teaching at the University of Freetown. He credited his pursuit of his doctorate to Marcus. Catherine believed Dr. Mensa was a good man. She was surprised to hear a rumor that he was considering taking a position with President Foday Payne.

Foday is smarter than people give him credit. Dr. Mensa will make him look legitimate.

The two men came over to the table.

"Ms. Catherine. It is wonderful to see you," Henry Koroma said.

He smelled of a heavy dosing of cologne. It was a habit that very few Africans or people working in Africa indulged in. When mixed with sweat, the effect was a sharp musky odor that was impossible to get out of the polyester suit he was wearing.

"It   :e to see you again, Mr. Henry. And you, Dr. Mensa?"

Dr. Mensa stepped forward. He extended his right arm toward her, held it at the elbow with his left hand, and bowed in a formal salute.

"It is my pleasure. I owe a great deal to your father. He is a great man," he said in Mende. "Please give him my regards." He spoke with refinement.

"We missed your father's input at the last ECOWAS meeting," Henry Koroma said as he and Dr. Mensa sat down. "Is he in Nigeria?" Henry Koroma smiled so wide his eyes closed. Catherine could literally count all his teeth.

"Yes. I'm sure he's sorry he missed it. I hope it was productive," she said. Needing to press for information, her energy returned.

"Indeed," Koroma replied.

"I suppose UN representatives were present?"

"Yes," Koroma said. He stopped smiling and glanced at Mensa. Catherine's probing put Koroma off. Women, no matter what their station, were never invited to these joint meetings, and the content of the discussions was not shared with them.

Celeste came back and sat down.

"And here is the mother-to-be," Koroma said jovially, attempting to change the subject.

Celeste beamed. "Hello."

"I'm curious about the meeting because when peacekeeping troops are deployed, the search for Mama will be stepped up, too" Catherine said, redirecting the conversation.

"I think that problem will be handled well then," Koroma responded. He stood up. Mensa stayed in his seat.

"What do you want to know, Ms. Catherine?" Mensa inquired.

"You both know about my relationship with Mama," Catherine said, looking from one to the other.

"Yes," Mensa said. Koroma remained silent. The smile melted from his face. He eyed Catherine. "The reason I'm here is because of her." Her voice cracked with emotion.

"Have you spoken with your father recently? I understand President Obasanjo has offered to help resolve this matter," Mensa said.

"It would give me peace of mind to know that her rescue is eminent."

Koroma cleared his throat, sending a warning signal to Mensa.

"The Nigerians will be in Liberia in two days," Mensa said. "Then we will see."

CHAPTER TWELVE

April 13, Later, Same Evening
Freetown Suburb

Lansana pulled up to a gate built into a stone wall and blew the horn. The gate opened a foot or so, and a young man about seventeen years old came out. He stood blinking into the headlights. "Come on, man, open the gate," Lansana shouted at his brother Kabbah, feigning annoyance.

"You be car and I be gate," the young man shouted back at him, grinning. Celeste smiled, entertained by the banter between the two brothers.

Jules and Celeste lived in a sprawling seven-bedroom rancher. It sat on a hill overlooking the Atlantic Ocean. Candles had been placed on the railings of the porch and along the path leading up to the door.

They had a staff of maids and groundkeepers, a cook and a driver. The aroma of baked chicken and fish and herb rice greeted her when she came through the front door into the living room. Soft light from lamps and the chandelier bathed the ivory sectional sofa, chairs, a massive gilded mirror standing against the wall, a dining room table imported from Spain, and gleaming tiled floors.

Celeste breezed through the rooms, headed toward the back of the house where Jules was waiting. On the terrace, a table was set for three.

"Hi, honey," Celeste said as she came up behind Jules. He was sitting on a lounge chair facing the ocean. She kissed him on the top of his head, then came around the chair, and stood over him. He reached up and gently placed his hand on her stomach. She placed her hand over his.

"Has the baby been active today?"

"Has he ever."

Celeste sat down on the lounge chair next to his. She threw her arms over the back of the chair and looked out at the choppy waves left behind by a tropical storm that was now making its way across the Atlantic, to North America.

"Where's Catherine?"

"She decided to go back to the hotel. Jet lag finally caught up with her."

"Was she all right?"

"I think so. Does she always push herself like that?"

"Yes. She's a lot like Marcus."

Celeste noticed that Jules was nervously twisting his wedding band. He did this when he was worried about something. He picked up the glass of lemonade from the small ornate table next to him and took a sip.

"How did the day go?" he said.

"Fine. I think I'm going to like hanging out with her."

Mendee came out of the house carrying a basket of bread covered with a blue batik napkin. She placed it carefully on the table then came over to Celeste.

"Would you like something to drink, Ms. Celeste?" she asked.

"Yes," Celeste said, "a glass of lemonade, please. No ice. Dinner can be served whenever it's ready. Mr. Coleman and I will be eating alone tonight. Ms. Catherine will join us for dinner some other time."

"Anything for you, Mr. Coleman?"

"Nothing right now."

Mendee turned and left.

"And how was your day?" said Celeste.

"Hectic," Jules replied, turning to face her. "I really wish she had stayed in the States until we had the situation with Madame Chief figured out. I have enough on my hands." Worry lines furrowed his forehead.

"I thought progress had been made."

"I wish. President Obasanjo gave Marcus his word that he would put his soldiers on it the minute they arrived in Liberia, but there's so much going on. President Taylor also said that his security staff would look for her. I know Marcus didn't like the idea of getting Taylor involved, but this thing has gone on too long."

"We ran into Koroma and Dr. Mensa today at the Paramount. That's exactly the same thing Dr. Mensa told Catherine."

"What did Catherine say?"

"Not much. She just seemed to take it in."

"I hope the Liberian soldiers don't find Madame Chief first," Jules said.

Celeste looked at Jules in disbelief. "Isn't rescuing her more important than who does it?"

"You know those boys. They're in a bad place, all drugged up and trigger-happy. If they foul this up and Madame Chief gets hurt . . . Maybe with Claypool Mensa around, they'll be cool. He's the new chief of border patrol, and he's what they call a real hands-on guy, if you know what I mean," Jules said sarcastically.

"Mensa's disciplinary tactics are disgusting," Celeste agreed.

"Well in this situation, it's better to have a Mensa around. If Madame Chief is accidentally killed in the cross fire, her people will go to war for sure. I'm just waiting for the other shoe to drop. We thought we had her. Taylor sent a search party to the last place she was reportedly seen, but she wasn't there. She could be anywhere in the bush by now."

The maid came back with a glass of lemonade and handed it to Celeste. "My that's good!" Celeste said after she drained the glass. She placed the cool glass against her forehead and rolled it back and forth.

"What's bothering you?"

"That gang of rebels that invaded the Kono district last year took over another diamond mine. We think Charles Taylor is helping them find buyers."

Celeste put the glass down and looked at Jules with sad eyes. "Did they leave anyone in the village alive?"

"Just enough people to work the mines," Jules remarked soberly. "That's another reason Marcus doesn't want to deal with Taylor. We really have to distance ourselves from him."

"I don't understand, Jules. Why doesn't Foday do something?"

"I don't know."

"What about the people they killed?"

"I know it looks like we're not paying attention, but we are. It's just one more thing in the list of problems. We'll get to it."

"I see why Catherine's so worked up about Mama," Celeste countered. "If it wasn't for Catherine, who knows when the international community would get around to Madame Chief."

Silence.

"Sierra Leone is in trouble, Celeste."

Celeste placed a hand on her stomach and looked at the lovely grounds around her home. "I don't want to talk about it."

A moment passed. "I told Catherine I would stop by tomorrow."

"How about the three of us going to breakfast? I want to see her face when she finds out that Benjamin is going to be her driver while she's here."

"I thought you were using one of the embassy regulars?"

"I changed my mind. With everything that's going on this week, I won't be able to keep track of her like I promised Marcus I would. Benjamin's a good man. He'll keep an eye on her. I'm glad you've decided to be her roadie."

"So I can spy on her," Celeste said with irritation.

"To keep an eye on her," Jules corrected.

"What do you think she'll do? She can't go anywhere except back to the States."

"I don't think she should go upcountry to Madame Chief's village," Jules replied.

"She wouldn't go without an escort, would she?"

"Probably not. But if she talks about leaving Freetown for any reason, I want to know. I wouldn't ask you to do it if I didn't have to. She's been full of surprises lately."

"Like coming back to Africa this month?"

"Something like that."

"I wonder if she knows how many people are looking out for her."

"I doubt that she's thought about it," Jules replied. "The only thing she seems to think about is Madame Chief's safety."

"You really worry about her, don't you?"

"Yes. The coup almost destroyed her." Jules looked directly at Celeste.

"Well, she seems all right to me now," Celeste offered gently.

"Catherine always seems all right to people who don't know her. Sooner or later, she's going to find out that the rebels holding Madame Chief may be headed toward Monrovia, which is why I want you to stay close to her. She's bound to make calls to the people she knows there."

"Like Claypool?"

"Maybe. Please don't tell her that Claypool Mensa is the new border chief in Liberia."

"Why not?"

"They went to International School together. He asked about her the last time I saw him."

"Could Claypool get her through the border block?"

"Probably, and just about anything else she might ask for. He has access to everyone and everything in Liberia."

"But he doesn't have any authority in Sierra Leone."

"No, but he has a lot of connections. I wish I knew him better. He might have been able to resolve this matter by now."

"Do you think he knows about Catherine's relationship with Madame Chief?"

"I have no idea."

"Maybe someone should tell him."

Jules thought for a moment. "Do me a favor. If Catherine so much as sneeze in Liberia's direction, let me know right away. OK? I may need to talk to him."

"I'll see if I can get her interested in doing a little volunteer work at the refugee camp," Celeste replied. "Give her something to do other than chasing down information about Madame Chief."

"It's worth a try."

"I'll run it by her tomorrow."

Jules stood up and helped Celeste up from the lounge chair. "I'm starving. Let's go eat."

"Catherine asked me about your trip to the refugee camp yesterday," Celeste remarked as they walked toward the dining area.

"Did you tell her about the letter that the doctor was carrying for her from Madame Chief?"

"No. I thought I'd let you do the honors."

CHAPTER THIRTEEN

April 13, Same Night
Lagos, Nigeria
Victoria Island

A driver from the US Embassy in Lagos and a security official carrying an AK-47 were waiting for Marcus when his plane arrived in Lagos from Abuja. He met them outside the terminal at the usual place.

The car was black with heavily tinted windows. The security officer sat in the front seat, holding his gun. He scanned the crowded streets of Lagos. As usual, traffic was New York City times ten. It took hours to get through. Bicyclers and pedestrians walked in the streets alongside cars, trucks, vans, and motorbikes. Hawkers selling food, clothes, sandals, cookware, and everything imaginable lined the bridges. Marcus was used to it. He busied himself in the backseat with the documents that had been generated that day. A boy came up alongside the car and attempted to look inside. He stepped back when the security official rolled down the window and waved him away.

Victoria Bridge, which crossed miles of water to Victoria Island, was heavily traveled. They crossed it in reasonable time. On the other side of the bridge, the landscape changed to middle-class homes, gated properties, stores, and restaurants. Here, the streets were also congested. They entered the area where the upscale district was located an hour later. Marcus put the documents away and gazed out the side window as the driver cruised slowly through the less-crowded streets. The houses of Gucci, Rolex, Armani, Versace, Cartier, and Prada were closing. Wealthy Nigerians were still inside buying merchandise. A man in a T-shirt, short pants, and flip-flops came out of the Rolex shop and began sweeping the dust from the entryway. Farther down the block, several men vigorously polished the metal doors to the Armani store. Banks with elaborate architectural features and beautiful sculptures at the entrance were closing. They passed Lexus, Mercedes, and Infinity car dealerships. Marcus observed a salesman handing the keys of a big silver Mercedes over to a Nigerian man and woman. On Victoria Island, amidst so much wealth, trash stood in the gutters, homeless men slept on the sidewalks, and traffic lights rarely work properly.

The driver pulled up to the Le Méridian, the hotel where Marcus always stayed when he came to Lagos. Le Méridian was a five-star hotel. Marcus preferred Le Méridian to the other four luxury hotels located in the same area despite its inefficient air-conditioning and poor air circulation. There was no particular reason for his preference except that the hotel had a good feeling to it, a homey feeling. Diplomats from Holland, Germany, France, and Japan also regularly checked in to Le Méridian. Marcus had noticed that the hotel was busier than usual, accommodating men in business suits who seemed to be everywhere. He surmised that the Nigerian oil market was active. Some of them looked young and eager. He had wondered if anyone had bothered to tell them which of the sixty banks within walking distance of Le Méridian to steer clear of. Half of them were run by Nigerian mobsters and scam artists.

"Good evening, Excellency," the clerk said as Marcus stopped at the registration desk in the reception area located outside the hotel.

"Good evening, Obadiah," Marcus responded. "Are there any messages for me?"

"I believe so, Excellency," the clerk said.

There was one from Catherine and one from Jules.

"I'm having dinner at the restaurant this evening. If anyone calls me, please direct the calls there."

"Of course, Excellency, I would be glad to."

As Marcus headed for the phone in the lobby, the president of the largest legitimate bank in Nigeria walked past him. His entourage of assistants, clerks, and vice presidents trailed behind him. He and Marcus nodded hello.

Marcus dialed the hotel operator and asked to be put through to the Bintumani. While he waited, he contemplated the list of tasks left undone, identified a few must dos, and placed them at the top of his list.

"Hotel Bintumani Hotel, how may I help you?" the desk clerk said.

"Catherine Lloyd's room please," Marcus replied.

"Certainly, sir."

Catherine picked up after nine rings.

"Daddy, how are you?" she said in a sleepy voice.

"I'm fine. How was your trip?"

"Fine, Daddy . . ." Her voice trailed off.

"I just called to say hello." Marcus realized that he had awakened Catherine, and there was no use attempting to hold a conversation with her. "We'll talk tomorrow."

"Sure, Daddy . . . ," Catherine responded. After a moment, Marcus heard her breathing. She had fallen back to sleep without hanging up. "Catherine? Catherine, wake up and hang up the phone."

"Oh OK, Daddy."

Click.

Marcus smiled as he thought about something his mother once said about Catherine. "She is definitely your child. She goes out like a light just like you, Marcus," she had said. "You could hang her over a clothesline, and she would go to sleep standing straight up." Marcus still wasn't sleeping more than four hours straight, but he took comfort in the thought that there was a time that he slept soundly. Suddenly it occurred to him that Catherine had arrived in Africa on the twelfth. Baffled, he could not imagine—particularly under the present circumstances—what had happened that had enabled her to do so. He pondered it and remembered that she was contemplating doing something different on the anniversary. He wondered if the two things were connected and decided to ask her about it when he saw her.

The Club Restaurant sat under an airy huge overhead enclosure. Fans with five-foot blades turned in the ceilings. A waiter led Marcus to a table directly under a ceiling fan. Marcus took a seat facing the street and the string of palm trees lining the sidewalk, swaying in the wind. It was the first time he had been able to sit and appreciate his surroundings all day.

A waiter came back and rattled off the specials adeptly. Several sounded interesting, but Marcus opted for the rice and chicken.

"Do you have one without spice?"

"We have made one with very little, sir."

"Good. I'll take it." Marcus thought about his stomach, and the amount of milk he had already consumed since the beginning of the week. He'd ordered it fresh from a farm less than a mile away because he did not trust the hotel's refrigeration.

Marcus opened his briefcase and took out a draft of the budget for moving the embassy to Abuja. He scoured the document line by line and penciled in suggestions to further upgrade the list of incentives and accommodations that had been recommended. Finished, he put the papers back in his briefcase.

A balmy evening breeze wafted through the eating area. His mind relaxed for a single moment until the problem of finding Madame Chief returned as it had done continuously throughout the day.

What bothered Marcus more than the fact that Madame Chief had not been rescued yet was that he still had not figured out the reason for her kidnapping. Marcus could not fathom why the rebels had not returned her by now. His experience had taught him that motive under similar situations had been lethal. He was contemplating the matter when something drew his attention, and he noticed Darryl Blopah sitting on the other side of the restaurant.

Blopah was Togolese. He had tribal markings on his cheeks and a French accent. He was in his early forties, but his slight build and youthful appearance made him look closer to thirty. He wore tailor-made clothes, a diamond in one ear, a Rolex, and a diamond-studded gold band on his left pinky.

Known throughout West Africa as a fixer, Blopah kept company only with the rich and powerful.

As with all fixers, no one actually knew how Blopah made his money. When queried about it, he righteously maintained that he was an entrepreneur. The latest rumor was that he was involved in insurance fraud, and that he had bilked several rich white people out of thousands of dollars. Many Africans looked up to Blopah, impressed with his acumen for such matters.

Blopah seemed to be keeping tabs on everyone coming into the restaurant. As guests passed, he casually eyed them from head to toe. Marcus was certain that Blopah knew he was there.

A man dressed in an expensive tailored suit came over to Blopah's table. Blopah stood and shook hands with him. Marcus watched with interest, thinking that Blopah might be the person he had been looking for, the one who could supply him with answers to his question about the kidnappers' motive. His gut instinct led him to conclude that they had one, that money was involved. He hesitated, then picked up his briefcase, and went over to Blopah's table.

"Good evening, Mr. Blopah."

With practiced movement, Blopah removed the napkin from his lap, touched the corners of his mouth, and wiped his hands. He adjusted his lapels as he stood up.

"Excellency, it is a pleasure to see you again." Blopah extended his hand. It was cool and dry.

"Would you mind if I joined you?" asked Marcus.

"Not at all," Blopah said, gesturing toward a chair.

"I see you have found your way back to Nigeria, Excellency," Blopah said smoothly.

"Indeed," Marcus replied.

"It is inevitable that our paths will cross. Do you not agree?"

"It seems that way," Marcus said with reluctance.

The waiter came back with water.

"How are things going for you?" Blopah inquired.

Marcus sensed that Blopah was well aware of some of the complications he was running into and that he was feeling him out, initiating some sort of mind game. The introduction of the game so quickly into their conversation surprised Marcus. It was sudden even for Blopah, who tended to move faster than most fixers, who usually took their time to size up their quarry.

"Very well, and you?" Marcus responded.

"Always good, Excellency," Darryl chuckled lightly. The markings on his cheeks danced.

Marcus said, making his own move, "Are you here on business or pleasure, Mr. Blopah?"

"Business, of course." Blopah chuckled again. "Isn't everyone in Lagos here on business? Hardly a place for touring is it? But the shopping is good."

The waiter returned and informed Marcus that the restaurant was out of the dish he had ordered.

"Try the veal marsala. It is exceptionally good this evening."

Blopah picked up his fork and knife, cut a piece of lamb, and delicately placed it in his mouth. He chewed it thoroughly, making a face that suggested culinary delight.

Although veal was not Marcus's idea of an alternative to chicken, he could ill afford to slight the man.

"I'll have the veal."

"Excellent choice." For a moment, Blopah almost appeared honest, but Marcus wasn't buying it. He was being frisked mentally. It wasn't what Blopah had said. It was something in his eyes.

I guess it's my move.

"Mr. Blopah, I was wondering if you are aware of the situation concerning Madame Chief."

Blopah ate another piece of veal, wiped his mouth, folded the napkin, and placed it on the table.

"I'm not sure I know what you mean," he answered, his tone edgy. "If you are asking me if I'm aware that Madame Chief was abducted by Liberian rebels several weeks ago, I am sure you know the answer to that question."

Marcus stared at him, sensing that he might have moved a little too fast and injured some sensibility. The waiter came back and took Blopah's plate. Blopah folded his hands on the table in front of him, leaned forward slightly, and looked directly at Marcus. "Everyone has heard about what happened to Madame Chief."

"It's the oddest thing," Marcus said, sensing an opening.

"Yes, I agree. I can't think of anything more ill-advised than kidnapping Madame Chief."

Marcus folded his hands on the table and mirrored Blopah's posture. "I have been coming up against a brick wall trying to find out who's benefiting from this. No one seems to know, or they're not talking."

Blopah gave Marcus a long, penetrating look.

The waiter returned with coffee, cream, and sugar. He lined up a spoon exactly an inch from the saucer and retreated. Blopah scooped a spoonful of coarse brown sugar out of a small ceramic bowl and slowly poured it into the coffee. He added cream until a patch of white bellowed to the surface of the dark brew.

"What makes you think there is anything more to the situation than what the newspapers and official report have indicated?" he said, slowing stirring the coffee.

"May I speak frankly?"

"Please, by all means. I am very interested in this conversation, and your opinions on this serious matter, Excellency."

"I wonder if you would give your opinion on whether the timing of her abduction was by plan or coincidence, or fate."

Blopah smiled slyly. "Fate! What an interesting word. Do you believe in fate, Excellency?" His eyes gleamed like a child's in a candy store. Marcus was intrigued. Blopah was engaging him in a philosophical debate.

"If you're asking me if I believe that fate plays a role in many things that seem to happen by chance, then the answer is yes," Marcus replied.

"Do you think it is fate that you and I should be guests in the same hotel, dining this evening at this particular restaurant?" Blopah asked with raised eyebrows.

"No."

"Why not?"

"Because you and I travel in some of the same circles, Mr. Blopah," Marcus contended.

"But what if it is fate?" Blopah shot back. "What if everything that has happened in our lives has been fated to happen, as you say, no accident, so that we could have this conversation tonight? Then all through our lives, the millions of decisions that we have made have been designed to lead us to this moment and to this table. *N'est pas?*"

Feeling uneasy, Marcus said, "Well, if that is the case, maybe we should get on with it."

Blopah grinned.

"But of course."

"I would be interested in hearing anything you can tell me about who's really behind Madame Chief's kidnapping."

Darryl sat back in his seat and smiled broadly. "You are one of the most interesting men I have ever met, Excellency," he said. "Everyone has a price, but you have always seemed to be an exception, or at least I thought so until today."

"Are you looking to get something out of this in exchange for information?"

"Oh, I would not even attempt to negotiate a price with you."

"And why is that, Mr. Blopah?" Marcus's eyebrows arched as he waited for the con.

"I am not so foolish as to put a dollar amount on supplying you with what you want to know," said Blopah. "As a matter of fact, the opportunity to converse with you in this way is worth a great deal to me."

Clearly, Blopah was in control of the game. Marcus wanted to walk away, but he thought of Catherine.

"Furthermore," Blopah continued, "I admire your integrity. It is clear to me that you are willing to deal with me only if it does not mean compromising your values. That, I believe, is where the line will be drawn because of your principles. If you cannot get what you are looking for from me without damaging your integrity, you will wait until it comes from one of your many other sources. So what do I really have to bargain with other than the possibility of shortening the waiting time?"

"I think you understand me well enough," Marcus said dryly.

"I am a very perceptive man, Excellency. And I have concluded that whatever is driving you to discuss this with me is a matter of the heart, and that cannot be bought and sold so easily."

Marcus shifted back in his chair. His fingers drummed the table for a moment.

"Fate is a strange thing," Blopah continued. "There is no reason for you to talk to me or I to you. But you see, it is this way—you are the only person I would want to tell what I know about Madame Chief's kidnapping. You are my hope for this godforsaken earth."

The waiter came back with a plate of veal and placed it in front of Marcus.

"Try it," Blopah urged. "I'm sure you will enjoy it as much as I did."

Marcus's stomach was churning, but he picked up the knife and fork, cut a small piece of the veal, and ate it. Blopah watched as he chewed the meat a few times. Marcus was surprised to find the food agreeable.

"There you see," Blopah said exuberantly, "we have more in common than you might think.

And now I will give you the piece of the puzzle you have been looking for. Several months ago, one of Minister Fofana's nephews asked me to serve as the intermediary between the minister and the leader of the LRFD. He originally told me that it was a minor deal, but that was of no interest to me. Large or small, my fee for such things is always the same. However, I did not know that the deal involved kidnapping Madame Chief." Blopah grunted in disgust. "When it came out that sixty thousand dollars was being paid to do it, I told Minister Fofana to find someone else for the job."

"Was anyone else involved in the deal?"

"Excellency, you seem to be fishing for evidence that would implicate someone else. Maybe, someone you have in mind?"

"I'm just covering all the bases," Marcus replied.

A man and woman entered the restaurant. The woman was an elegantly dressed African. Judging from his suit, the man appeared to be European. Blopah's eyes followed them across the room; then he checked his watch.

"It is getting late, and I have to leave early in the morning to meet with a client." The smile had disappeared from his face. He signaled the waiter for the check. "It was a pleasure spending time with you this evening. Until our paths cross again, I wish you well. Please give my regards to your daughter, Catherine. I hope her stay in Sierra Leone is everything she hopes it will be."

With that, Blopah hastily stood up, intercepted the waiter, signed the check, and left the restaurant.

Well I'll be damned.

Blopah had made sure Marcus would remember their chance meeting. He had played a trump card by mentioning Catherine. Marcus wondered how he had found out so quickly she was in Sierra Leone. Blopah had made his point, his intention was clear. He was in control of the game.

CHAPTER FOURTEEN

April 14
Freetown

Catherine was riding the crest of a wave that set her down on the sand near a coconut grove when her dream was interrupted by the incessant ringing of a telephone.

"Hello?" She held the phone to her ear and rolled back on the pillow with her eyes still closed. The roar of rolling tides washing up on the shore lingered a little longer and then dissolved.

"Good morning, Catherine." It was Jules.

"Hi, Jules."

She sat up and looked at the clock. It was 8:00 a.m. She had slept twelve hours.

"Did I wake you?"

"Yes, but that's OK. Did you find Mama yet?"

Jules hesitated. "Not exactly."

"Meaning?"

"How about meeting us for breakfast so I can give you an update?"

"What time?"

"How about ten?"

"I'll meet you in the lobby."

Catherine hung up then turned on the shortwave radio she had brought with her. The jingle signaling the African news was playing. The first report was on Liberia.

"A battle between rebels and Liberian soldiers took place on the docks of Monrovia early this morning," the reporter said. "Several civilians were killed, and others were injured. A shipment of medical supplies was severely damaged. The medicine was earmarked for the refugee camps, and the next shipment is not expected for several weeks. A representative from the UN stated that ECOMOG peacekeeping troops are scheduled to begin arriving tomorrow."

Catherine turned off the radio and glanced at the clock. The report had triggered restlessness.

Where are you, Mama? I've got to get out of here.

She decided to run.

A blast of warm air hit Catherine in the face as she came through the door. She opened a bottle of water. While she walked, she drank half of it. She turned onto a dusty road and jogged slowly toward a residential area. A group of schoolchildren fell in step with her. They were curious about a foreign woman running, not driving, on the road. She smiled at them then quickened her pace.

When she returned to her room, Catherine showered and dressed. It had been a good run. The restlessness had been conquered. Restored, she sat on the deck and looked out at the ocean, musing about the rebels and Madame Chief.

She was about to go meet Jules when the phone rang.

"Hey, girl."

"Justine!"

"I got tired of waiting to hear from you. How's it goin'?"

The comfort of Justine's voice reached out and hugged Catherine.

"Fine, just fine," she said.

"I'm not going to keep you. Just wanted to hear your voice," Justine said. "You sure you're OK?"

"Yes. It's so good hearing from you. I wish I could stay to talk, but I'm meeting Jules for breakfast. He wants to talk. I'll give you a call tonight when I get back to the hotel. Promise."

"I have to tell you something before you leave."

"OK."

"You'll never believe what I did."

"What?"

"I bought a shortwave radio."

"Get out of here! Not you!" Catherine said and chuckled.

"It was Harold's idea. He thought I might like to know what's going on in your part of the world."

"Thank Harold for me, will you?"

"And Clifton said to tell you hello!"

"How is he?" Catherine said and smiled softly.

"He stopped by to play pool. I overheard him ask Harold if I had talked to you and if I knew who was meeting you at the airport when you came back. What should I tell him?"

"Tell him I miss him too."

"OK. I'll talk to you later."

"Caio, Justine." Catherine thought about the last time she saw Clifton, the way his eyes had scanned her face and hair when they'd said good-bye. She debated whether or not to call him. She checked her watch and sighed. *Perhaps later.*

When she reached the lobby, she saw Samuel Rogers-Clark standing at the reception desk.

Born in Sierra Leone, Samuel was the son of a paramount chief. Commandingly handsome, he had been educated in the United States after graduating from the International School. It was widely accepted that one day Samuel would run for president of Sierra Leone.

When Samuel first met Catherine at the International, he simply nodded; and after that, as he did all foreigners, he kept his distance from her until he heard her speaking Mende and found out that Madame Chief was her benefactor. The year she went to live in Liberia, he had inquired about where she had gone when she did not return to the International School in the fall.

As Catherine approached Samuel to say hello, it dawned on her that of all the men she knew in Sierra Leone, Samuel was probably the only one who might be willing to help her hire mercenaries. The idea made her feel hopeful. She could barely restrain the impulse to ask him straight out if he would help her.

"Good morning, Samuel."

Samuel turned and smiled. "Good morning, Catherine." He didn't seem surprised to see her. He kissed her on both cheeks. "How have you been?"

"I've been well. And you?"

"Quite well."

"How are your parents?"

"They are well. And your father?"

"He's fine."

How should I bring it up? Even though they were friends, he was an African man.

"What are you up to this morning?" she asked inst

"Not much. Just working. How about you?"

"I'm meeting Jules and Celeste for breakfast.

us?"

A breakfast buffet w

"Sounds good

"How ab

"N

the great hall leading from the

situated to the left and right of the

prized attractions—the ocean and the co

a view of Lumley Beach.

Catherine noticed a woman dressed as Mad

dressed if she was meeting Catherine for brea

reading her mind, Jules reached into an inside po

took out an envelope. "This is from Madame Ch

it to her.

"How did you get this?" Stunned, Catherine

opened it.

"The doctor who treated her gave it to me.

camps. She asked him to make sure I got it

you."

Excited, Catherine opened the ruled paper.

"Sorry, I can't. I'm meeting someone."

"Too bad. Maybe some other time," Catherine said.

Samuel studied Catherine intently. "I assume you're staying here."

"But of course. You know how much I love this hotel."

"I'll give you a call. Better still, let me give you my card." He reached into the breast pocket of his jacket. "Give me a call when you want to get together."

A man carrying an attaché case stepped out of the elevator and came toward them.

"I'd like to stay and talk for a while, but I've got to go," Samuel said, looking in the man's direction.

He took Catherine's hand and kissed the back of it. "Call me when you're free," he said and walked away.

Damn, I should have asked him!

Madame Chief's maid, Ester, came into the lobby with the stranger Celeste had referred to as Fofana's flunky the night before. She looked around nervously. She turned away when she saw Catherine.

What's Ester doing here with him?

Ester and the man ducked into a room and closed the door.

It's probably nothing, Catherine thought, but she couldn't get the look on Ester's face out of her mind.

Jules and Celeste entered the lobby.

"Hey, Catherine," said Jules, beaming. He kissed Catherine on both cheeks. "You look rested."

"How are you feeling this morning?" Celeste asked with a concerned look on her face.

"Better. Much better," Catherine replied. She glanced at the door Ester and the man had disappeared into. "I just saw Madame Chief's maid with that creepy guy we saw last night," she said, nodding in the direction of the room.

"What's Ester doing with him?"

Celeste made a face as if she had just tasted something foul.

"I have no idea," Celeste said, looking in the direction of the door.

Jules took Catherine by the arm. "I have a little surprise for you." He led her toward the front door.

When they got outside, Benjamin was standing next to a sedan. He waved when he saw Catherine.

"I asked Benjamin to be your driver until Madame Chief comes back."

"Thank you, Jules!"

"My pleasure, little sister. So where would you like to have breakfast?"

"How about here?"

"Sounds good to me."

A breakfast buffet was spread out on a banquet-size table at the end of the great hall leading from the lobby to the dining area. Dining rooms were situated to the left and right of the hall, each offering a view of Freetown's prized attractions—the ocean and the countryside. They choose one with a view of Lumley Beach.

Catherine noticed a woman dressed as Madame Chief might have dressed if she was meeting Catherine for breakfast that day. As if reading her mind, Jules reached into an inside pocket of his jacket and took out an envelope. "This is from Madame Chief," he said, handing it to her.

"How did you get this?" Stunned, Catherine took the envelope and opened it.

"The doctor who treated her gave it to me. He's working in the refugee camps. She asked him to make sure I got it so that I could send it to you."

Excited, Catherine opened the ruled paper. The letter was dated April 4.

My dearest Catherine:

I pray this letter finds you well. Please forgive me for not contacting you earlier to let you know that I would not be able to come to see you this year.

By the time you receive this letter, I suspect the anniversary will have passed. I believe with all my heart that you have fared it well. I have watched you grow stronger with each passing year, preparing for the day I would not be able to walk with you on the 12th. You were in my prayers that day.

Needless to say, I have never been in such a strange position. I would like to think that it will be over by the time you receive this letter. In the event it is not, I am not worried, and neither should you be. My people will come for me soon.

It is a beautiful day today. Not too hot. There is a cloudless sky above me, nothing to slow down the prayers that I send up to God.

Take care of yourself. We will have much to talk about when I return to Sierra Leone.

With sincere love,
PC Madame Victoria Palmer-Shaw

Catherine read the letter again. It was a bittersweet moment, a mixture of joy and yearning. Her worst fears were momentarily pushed to the side.

"What's wrong with Mama?" she asked, looking over at Jules.

"What do you mean?" he replied, stalling. It wasn't the reaction he had expected. Catherine's eyes flashed.

"She's fine. The rebels are doing a good job of taking care of her."

"Answer the goddamn question, Jules."

Jules hesitated.

"She has a heart condition."

"She has a what?" Catherine's voice rose. "And you kept that from me?"

"The doctor said she responded well to the medication, and he left her all he had."

"And how much was that?"

"Enough for two weeks, maybe a little more."

"So a conservative estimate is that she has enough for four more days."

"He's not the only doctor in Liberia, Catherine," Jules said with annoyance. "They found him, and I'm sure they'll find another one."

Catherine turned to Celeste. "What do you think? You know how many doctors there are in the area."

Celeste hesitated. "I think Jules may be right," she said, looking uncomfortable.

Catherine stood up. "I have to go back to my room. There's someone I want to call," she said, thinking about Samuel and the mercenaries. "I'll be back."

CHAPTER FIFTEEN

April 14
Later that Evening

Samuel had agreed to meet her at eight.

Catherine was dressed to the nines. Before leaving the hotel, Jules had invited her to a birthday party for Edward Reynolds, the US ambassador to Sierra Leone. The party was at 6:00 p.m. Samuel arrived dressed in a dark brown political suit with polished gold buttons.

"I hope you won't mind if I tell you that you look lovely," Samuel said when he saw her.

"Not at all," said Catherine, accepting the compliment.

"Let's go to the casino," Samuel suggested.

"Still betting?"

"Not lately, I'm tired of losing. But I still like the atmosphere."

Samuel offered Catherine his arm, and she hooked hers around it.

The night air was balmy. A full moon lit the stone path that went through the gardens, past a pool with colored lights shimmering below the surface of the water, to the casino.

A white woman, barefoot and dressed in a floor-length black sequined gown, appeared on the path. Her shoulder-length platinum hair was luminous in the night. As she passed, she gave Samuel the once-over. He nodded.

"Who's that?" Catherine asked, always curious about Caucasians who appeared comfortable in Africa.

"She is a diamond dealer from Belgium," Samuel replied. "She has five children. A couple of them are nearly our age."

"Is she legitimate?"

"Very legitimate."

The garden opened to a sidewalk and a busy street. Cabs lined the curb. Some of the drivers leaned against their cars, while others talked with one another while waiting for customers. A crippled beggar came toward Catherine and Samuel with his hand out. His legs bent inward at the knees, touching slightly. He waddled and bobbed as he dragged his feet along the ground. Catherine went in her purse, pulled out twenty leones, and handed them to him. She wondered if he had been born handicapped, or if his limbs had been broken on purpose so that he could bring in money to the family. She decided it was the latter. She had seen it many times before.

The Bintumani's casino was carpeted and about the size of a ballroom. Blackjack tables, wheels of fortune, and dice tables sat in the center of the room. A bar was to the left. Slot machines lined the back wall. A black door in the back opened to a room for high rollers.

A man rolling dice at the craps table had attracted a crowd. He shook the dice, blew on them, and released them. The people cheered.

They took a booth. Catherine ordered a glass of wine. A devout Muslim, Samuel ordered a soda. "So when was the last time you were in the States?" Catherine asked, opening with light conversation.

"It's been awhile. I went to New York to see my brother about two years ago. Are you still teaching in Philadelphia?"

"Yes."

"Do you like it there?"

"It's fine."

"Do you ever miss living in Africa?"

"Yes, why do you ask?"

"No reason. Just wondering. I suppose you've heard about Mama."

"Of course. That's why I'm here."

Even in the dim light, Catherine saw a shadow pass briefly over his face.

"So what's up?" asked Samuel after a moment. "You were pretty vague when you called me, and that's not like . . ."

Samuel stopped talking. Catherine turned to see what had caught his attention. Richard Acolatse had come through the door with a tall, slender woman. The woman's hair was cut close. She wore a white evening gown and large gold earrings.

"Merde!"

"You have something against Ricky?"

"Not yet, but he seems to be working on it."

"Ricky's OK. His dad and mine have a few business ventures they're trying to get off the ground."

"Really? What about his other ventures," Catherine said with disapproval.

"I'm talking to him about that. Give him a chance."

Samuel stood up as Richard and his companion approached. They hugged, clasped hands, and snapped fingers as they drew them apart.

"Good evening, Ms. Catherine. We just seem to keep running into each other," Richard said. The woman leaned against him suggestively and stared at Catherine with sensuous large eyes. "She is very pretty," she said to Richard in French. From her accent, Catherine could tell she was Senegalese. Richard nodded in agreement.

"May I introduce Alise?" Richard said to Catherine.

"Good evening," Catherine responded in English deliberately.

Samuel jumped in. "So what are you up to tonight?"

"Just showing Alise Sierra Leone's nightlife."

"Why don't you join us?"

"We would love to, but we've already kept our friends waiting." Richard nodded in the direction of a couple seated at a table not far away.

The waiter arrived with a glass of wine for Catherine and soda for Samuel. "Let me get that for you," Richard interjected before Samuel could reach into his pocket. He took out a roll of money, peeled off a few large bills, and handed them to the waiter.

Catherine nodded in lukewarm appreciation.

Richard bowed slightly from the waist. "It is always a pleasure to see you, Ms. Catherine. Take care of her, Samuel. She's a nice lady." Richard smiled. His face was soft, almost nice. Almost.

After Richard and the woman retreated, Samuel spoke. "How long are you planning to stay in Sierra Leone?"

"I suppose I'll be here until Mama comes home."

"Let me give you a bit of advice. Don't travel in the bush until the ECOMOG soldiers are in place," he warned. "They've already begun arriving, and the situation in Liberia will be in control while they're there. I think they plan to make finding Mama their top priority as soon as they get situated." Samuel paused. "I hope you don't have any plans to go to Liberia?"

"It hadn't crossed my mind."

"Well if it does, get in touch with Claypool before you go. He's the new chief of border security in Liberia."

"Are you talking about Claypool Mensa?"

It was hard for Catherine to imagine Claypool as chief of border security. He had been the class clown and had almost been kicked out of the International School because of his antics. Big and burly, Catherine had nicknamed him Double O when they first met. He worked on the rolls of fat and turned them into muscle by the end of their senior year. After that, the boys at school called him Double O Seven.

"The Claypool I know was always looking for a way to have a little fun. I just can't imagine him with a serious job. How did he find out that we knew each other?"

"I was in Liberia for a meeting with Charles Taylor. Claypool and I started talking, and we discovered we had both attended the International Schools. One thing led to another, and your name came up. He told me that after they rescue Mama, they're bringing her back to Monrovia. With communication the way it is, it may be several days before the word gets to us. You should call Claypool and let him know you're here. He'll personally call you when they bring her in."

When Catherine went back to her room, she turned the BBC. The African news was already in progress. She listened as she undressed for bed.

"The attack on Monrovia by LRFD rebels who backed out of the ECOWAS-brokered ceasefire last Tuesday has left Monrovia and its more than one million occupants bewildered. ECOMOG peacekeeping troops have begun arriving and are expected to quell the situation over the next few days. The UN is providing aid to civilians. The city is without electricity. Water supplies have been contaminated. A spokesperson for the UN said that efforts are being made to clean up the water as quickly as possible to prevent the spread of disease. Health problems continue to mount as workers report severe cases of diarrhea and malaria among an estimated 50,000 internally displaced persons living at the D. Twe and G. W. Gibson High Schools in central Monrovia. A new shipment of medical supplies is expected by the end of the week. There are also reports that peacekeeping forces met heavy resistance from two rebel armies that have become entrenched in the outskirts of Monrovia."

Catherine turned off the radio. She sat thinking, her arms around her knees. *What made ECOWAS and the UN think the rebels would honor a truce? Why should they? What are they getting out of it? Mama's sick and those boys are crazy . . . They'll use every man and boy-soldier they have to fight ECOMOG.*

Uncertainty played with Catherine's mind. *When will ECOMOG have time to look for Mama?* Doubt weighed on her. *Samuel and Dr. Mensa are speculating.*

She thought about hiring mercenaries.

The stories she had heard about the CIA and the Nigerians' wet work and other questionable covert operations were clear in her mind. They were Catherine's last thoughts before turning out the light.

Catherine was in a basement. Something appeared in a dark corner and scurried along the base of the wall. Catherine raised a rifle and waited. The animal stepped into the light. It was a beautiful greyhound dog, lean and graceful, built for speed and championship ribbons. She lowered the gun cautiously. Suddenly the hair on the back of her neck rose. Quickly she took aim and shot the dog between the eyes. It fell to the ground and morphed into a huge rat, with long sharp teeth and claws.

Catherine sat straight up and turned on the light.

A voice inside her head said, *A rat is a rat no matter how it changes its appearance.*

Catherine gathered her thoughts. The rat in her subconscious was human. The rat in the dream was Richard Acolatse.

Her gut told her that Richard was involved in Madame Chief's kidnapping. But she knew that there was no way to prove it.

CHAPTER SIXTEEN

April 15
Robertsport, Liberia

The house was built like an American Southern mansion but on a slightly smaller scale. Four large white pillars braced the entrance, and a porch wrapped around the front. The acre of land surrounding the house had been cleared away on three sides. The house faced a long road that went over a small hill, connected to a narrow road through the bush, then finally led to a main road. Old jeeps—dusty, dented, and missing doors—sat in front of the house and along the road. Rebels in ragtag uniforms loitered around the vehicles or sat idly, doing drugs under shade trees. A hundred and twenty-five to approximately five hundred LRFD rebels roaming the villages outside of Monrovia were stationed at the house. A quarter of the LRFD were boy-soldiers.

Mohamed came into the bedroom where Madame Chief was sleeping and gently touched her arm. "Mama, Mama," he said softly.

Madame Chief's back was to him, but she sensed his excitement. She turned over. Mohamed stepped back, creating a respectful distance between them.

Bright morning light spilled into the pleasantly decorated room.

"What time is it?" Madame Chief inquired.

"It is seven twenty-five."

"So early?"

"There is something I must tell you," Mohamed said.

"What is it?"

"Someone is coming to talk to you about going back to Sierra Leone today."

Madame Chief's eyes stretched wide with disbelief, then narrowed.

"Who told you this?"

"Aaron Sir."

Madame Chief paused to consider whether to trust the information or not. *Why now? Is it possible?*

"Is there still fighting going on?"

"Yes, Mama. It is fierce."

The clashes between rebel groups fighting for control of Liberia had made movement from one place to another unsafe. Mama was convinced that if Blaze had not been with her during the two skirmishes over the forty miles between Tubmanburg and Robertsport, she probably would have been dead by now. Consequently, she was more than a little curious about how the people Mohamed was talking about planned to keep her out of harm's way over the hundreds of miles back to Sierra Leone.

Mohamed looked around for the envelope holding Madame Chief's nitroglycerine tablets.

"Here, take one of these." He handed her the envelope. Madame Chief sat up and waved it away.

"I will take it later."

She swung her legs carefully over the side of the bed. Mohamed held her arm as she stood up and went to a chair near the window.

"I am glad that I was the one chosen to bring you this news," Mohamed said. His eyes were sad.

I will miss you too if this is the day.

They heard Blaze talking to someone in the hall.

"I have to speak with Blaze," Mohamed said, urgency in his voice. He started toward the door. "I will send a girl to help you get dressed."

Madame Chief looked around the room that she had occupied for five days. Pink and white with frilly curtains, it had been decorated for a little girl. There was a handmade African doll sitting on a white wicker chest in one corner. Madame Chief wondered how it had come to be left behind.

There was a soft knock on the door.

"Come in."

The door opened slowly, and a girl about fifteen years old stepped into the room. She had thin knobby knees. She waited timidly for permission to approach.

"Come, come," said Madame Chief, motioning for her to move closer.

She was wearing a dress meant for a younger girl. It pulled tightly around her small breasts, the sleeves puckered under her armpits, and the waist sat high up.

"Good morning, Mama," she said, looking down at the floor.

This one was different from the other girls Mohamed had sent to attend to her. They had been the liveliest and most confident of the plain-looking girls who cooked and cleaned and visited the rebels in their beds. Mohamed called them the cheery ones. He thought they helped keep Madame Chief's spirits up. He never sent the pretty girls who dressed seductively and did little more than sleep with the men who were higher up in rank. They tended to be chatty and undisciplined.

Madame Chief had never seen this girl before. Her hair stood out in every direction as if it had not been combed in weeks. One side of her face was puffy and bruised. Her condition disturbed Madame Chief greatly.

"What is your name?" Madame Chief asked gently.

"My name is Alice."

Madame Chief lifted the girl's chin. The girl's sad eyes averted while Madame Chief examined her injury.

"Who did this to you?"

The girl dropped her head and stared at the floor.

"How long have you been here?"

Alice looked up. Her eyes grew large and wild. "I was taken from my village by the soldiers three days ago. Or was it four," she said. Seeming confused, she fastened her eyes on the floor again.

Madame Chief lifted the girl's chin again and forced her to look at her.

"No one will hit you again," she said. "But I must know who is responsible for this."

The maid's eyes went blank.

There was a hard knock on the door. Alice winced.

"Come in," said Madame Chief, annoyed by the interruption.

Aaron strolled into the room. Alice backpedaled into a corner and hit the wall hard. Aaron shot a hard look at her. She cringed.

"Alice was just about to help me get dressed."

Aaron turned and stared at Madame Chief. "I can send someone else," he said. His nostrils flared, and the veins in his neck pulsed. He reminded Madame Chief of a dog whose bone had been taken. He turned and started toward Alice. She whimpered and threw her arms up to fend him off. Now there was no question who had beat her.

"I prefer this girl," Madame Chief said firmly. "Now if you don't mind, I would like to get dressed." She glared at Aaron. "Come to me, Alice."

She held out her hand. Alice looked from Madame Chief to Aaron.

"Come now. I have things to do."

Alice slid past Aaron, eyes wide, bracing for a blow. She stood behind Madame Chief.

The anger twisting Aaron's face faded. He smiled cynically.

"Is there something else, Aaron?" Madame Chief asked.

"Yes, there is."

"What is it?"

"You have been asking many questions, but for all your efforts, you know very little, only what I have wanted you to know."

"Is there a point to this?" Madame Chief asked with contempt.

"I know that you have discovered that my last name is Fofana. I am also sure that you have figured out who my uncle is. When you return to your village, you will find that certain changes have taken place while you were away. My uncle has obtained the signatures of two of your subchiefs to begin mining . . . for diamonds."

What?

Tension exploded in the muscles along Madame Chief's shoulders as her mind raged. Her eyes narrowed. Her gaze pierced him.

"My uncle instructed me to tell you to expect this so that the surprise would not put too much strain on your heart."

"How generous," Madame Chief remarked dryly. "I will have to thank him when I see him."

"Would you like to know how we found out about the diamonds?"

"Not especially."

"It was your maid, Ester, who brought the diamonds to my uncle's attention. How long was she your maid? Ah yes, twenty-five years, I believe. She will not be at your house when you return. My uncle thought it best." His eyebrows arched in derision. "Your personal maid, Nadia, cried so hard when she found out that Ester had betrayed you, she became sick and had to be taken to the hospital."

"Then it is best that Ester be gone before I return," Madame Chief responded. Sadness pressed heavily on her heart. For the first time in her life, she felt defeated. She had failed to protect her village.

When she left the room, Alice followed behind her like a baby duckling. Rebels nodded as she passed them, but Madame Chief did not return their greeting.

Every morning, Madame Chief sat on the porch in a rocking chair Mohamed had placed there for her. When she was there, it was her domain, and no one lingered there without her permission. From this vantage point, she observed the rebels, watching those who seemed unhappy, somber, or scared. They had been forced to join the LRFD. She invited these boys to come and talk to her. She talked to them about the day Liberia would elect a president, uniting the country again. She encouraged them to survive. As for the ones who had voluntarily joined the rebels, those who so easily shot and hacked helpless villagers to death for "the cause," she challenged them to defend their ideology. They could not of course. These conversations were short, but she always made her point.

The day after Madame Chief had come to the camp, she discovered a well-worn path through the bush. She walked it several times a day, through tropical flowers and berry bushes. The wind of the path brought Catherine to mind. She would have preferred to walk alone, but Mohamed, Joe, or Blaze went with her everywhere.

She was considering taking a walk to clear her head when Mohamed and Blaze tumbled out the door and onto the porch, laughing and pushing each other. Blaze wore a brand-new bright red wig. He strutted over to Madame Chief, grinning and pointing to the hairpiece.

"How do you like it?" he said, bending over. Madame Chief eyed it for a moment. "It is a much better wig than the last one," she finally responded. Blaze clapped his hands. "There, I told you she would like it," he said, turning to Mohamed.

Blaze turned to Madame Chief. The smile was gone from his face. It seemed as if he had something important to say. Mohamed nudged him in the side in an effort to get him to speak.

"Mama . . . ," Blaze began, referring to her affectionately for the first time.

"Yes, Blaze."

He hesitated and glanced sideway at Mohamed. Mohamed nodded encouragement. Blaze reached up under the wig and scratched his head.

"Mama, Blaze has decided to stop sniffing the drugs," Mohamed interjected impatiently.

"Is this true, Blaze?"

"Yes, Mama," Blaze said. His eyes gleamed with pride. "I want you to bless me, Mama. To help me," he said, kneeling.

Madame Chief pushed her hand under Blaze's wig and began to pray softly. Under a nearby tree, a group of soldiers stopped talking and watched. After a moment, a few scowled and walked away. Their interest in spiritual matters had been destroyed long ago.

Madame Chief raised her voice. "Heavenly Father, bless this boy who comes to you now, who has heard your son, Jesus Christ, calling."

Suddenly Aaron came around the side of the house. Two rebels wearing brightly colored wigs and bras over their T-shirts followed close behind. He stopped and shot a menacing look at Mohamed. Mohamed held his ground. Aaron said something to the two men with him, and they laughed.

"Move!" he barked at the soldiers, watching Madame Chief and Blaze. "Go about your business." He ran up to one and kicked him in the butt as they began to disperse. Madame Chief prayed louder.

"Bless this boy. Forgive his sins. Smile down on him, Heavenly Father, and give him peace."

Aaron and the two rebels jumped in a jeep and sped recklessly down the road, throwing dust and pebbles into the faces of the men sitting alongside it.

Blaze stood. "That was good, Mama." He looked up at the sky and smiled. "This is a good day. Thank you, Mama." Blaze picked up his gun and jumped down off the porch. He raised a fist and the AK-47 jubilantly above his head. A few of his comrades came back and met him, laughing and patting him on the back. Exuberant, Blaze shot off a round of bullets in the air. Madame Chief sighed.

"Would you like to go for a walk this morning?" Mohamed asked.

"No, I don't think so, Mohamed," she replied. "I think I will stay here."

Madame Chief took her seat and gazed at the road. *Maybe I still have time to change things.*

CHAPTER SEVENTEEN

April 16
Freetown

Anxious, Catherine glanced at her watch and checked to see who was coming through the door of the hotel lobby for the third time in fifteen minutes. As if on cue, Benjamin appeared in the doorway carrying a large brown paper bag. He moved with purpose to Catherine, a faint smile was on his face.

He handed her the bag. She opened it. It was filled with four thousand leones, the equivalent of two hundred American dollars, and a small handgun.

"Thank you, Benjamin," Catherine said. She took a deep breath, rolled the bag closed, and stuffed it inside the small *kente* valise she had purchased in town.

"You are very welcome."

"Did you find enough petro for the trip?"

"Yes, Ms. Catherine. There is plenty of petro."

Her spur-of-the-moment plan to drive the five hours to the border, stay overnight at the Coconut Grove Hotel on the Sierra Leone side, then pass through checkpoints—now in position every ten miles—had cost her three times the going price for gas. They would have to hurry to arrive at the hotel before sunset.

Before deciding to go to Liberia, Catherine had asked Marcus about the progress being made to bring Madame Chief back home, and the news had not been good. The UN had sent one of their representatives to negotiate Madame Chief's release, but they never reached the rebel headquarters. Marcus had not told Catherine that their cars were found with a note attached to the steering wheel demanding money for their return. Instead, he'd said, "The plan fell through." Claypool told her about the ransom note.

Claypool had no reservations about helping Catherine hire mercenaries. "If this thing is done, His Excellency President Taylor will have one less thing to be concerned about," he'd said. Afterward, he sent her traveling papers overnight by courier, with assurance that his men—as well as the Ghanaian, Guinean, Nigerian, and Senegalese soldiers at the different checkpoints—would allow her to pass through the checkpoint without any trouble as long as she carried them. "Like magic," he'd said with a chuckle, "the door will open."

Initially, the idea of carrying a gun made Catherine feel crazy, but the feeling gave way when she thought about herself and Benjamin traveling alone without one.

"How hard could it be to shoot this?" she had said to Benjamin.

"It is not the shooting that be hard. It is the killing," he'd replied.

"Show me."

Immediately after she made the decision to go to Liberia, the stories about Liberian rebels became more real than she had allowed them to be before. They awakened images of the drunken, raging soldiers who had murdered her friends, and they filled her dreams. She realized how wise it had been to stay away from Liberia.

Catherine reached for the locket hanging around her neck that held Madame Chief's picture and squeezed it. "OK, let's go," she said.

The head clerk waved as Catherine and Benjamin passed. Catherine had left a letter for Celeste. He had promised to deliver it as soon as she was gone. In the letter, Catherine had promised to call when the telephone lines were operating again.

"I wish I could have seen Celeste to say good-bye," she confided in Benjamin as they walked toward the door.

They stepped outside into hot, blinding sun. Catherine put on her sunglasses. "Do we have enough water?"

"There is plenty."

Benjamin put the suitcase in the trunk.

"The car will be cool soon," he added as they got in. Catherine was already sweating profusely. She took a bottle of water from the case sitting on the seat next to her and drank it. There was another case on the floor. As Benjamin put the car in gear, Celeste pulled into the driveway. She waved at Catherine.

"Right," Catherine muttered under her breath. She put on her best "I'm so glad to see you" smile.

Celeste opened the car door, pushed the case of water over, and got in.

"Hey. Where you goin'?"

"Just out for a ride." Catherine held the smile firmly in place.

"A ride? Where to?"

"Nowhere in particular."

"Mind if I come along?"

Celeste began to pull the seat belt over her protruding stomach. "I'm starving. Let's get something to eat. There's one other—"

"You can't go with me," Catherine blurted.

"Why not?"

Catherine hesitated, debating whether or not to tell the truth.

"You're leaving town, aren't you?"

"What makes you think that?"

Celeste chuckled. "Spies." She turned and waved to the doorman who waved back.

"Monrovia, right?"

"How did you find out so fast?"

"I had to stop by the embassy. I was talking to Jules's secretary who happened to mention that Benjamin had signed out the car to go to Monrovia. I called the hotel to see if you were still in your room. It wasn't hard to figure it out after that. You've been talking to Claypool, haven't you?"

The smile fled from Catherine's face. "You sound like Jules," she said with distrust. "Where is he anyway? Out of town? Did he tell you to keep an eye on me?"

"I, uh . . ."

Annoyed, Catherine turned and stared out the window.

Celeste took a bottle of water out of the case and sipped it. Slowly a crafty smile came to her face. "What do you think of the idea of skipping the roadblocks?"

"How?" Catherine said, turning to face her.

Celeste pointed to the sky.

"You mean fly to Liberia? I've already thought of that. Robertsfield is closed down."

"How about a private helicopter?"

"There aren't any available. I checked."

"One is coming in from Monrovia in about an hour."

Celeste explained that a pilot had been hired by the Catholic Relief Services to bring in some of their people working in Liberia.

"He's going to Lungi Island to fuel up and then back to Liberia. His name is Robert Latimore, but we call him Bobby. You can hitch a ride with him."

"Where's he landing?"

"Right here, behind the Bintumani," Celeste replied.

CHAPTER EIGHTEEN

The Landing

Catherine and Celeste watched a helicopter coming toward the Bintumani.

"He stopped drinking for the most part," Celeste said to Catherine after she told her that Bobby had been a pilot for England's Royal Air Force but had drank too much and cashed out.

Catherine looked askance at Celeste. *You've got to be kidding.*

"He used to fly for African dictators, but about fifteen years ago, he began flying for emergency humanitarian relief efforts in the Sudan, Ethiopia, the Congo, and lately Liberia for little or no money."

Catherine studied Bobby's short-cropped white hair and angular features as he set the helicopter down and got out.

"Come with me," Celeste said to Catherine and Benjamin. Catherine fell in step behind her, pushing aside her questions about the wisdom in flying with Bobby.

After the last passenger got off, Bobby took a cigar out of his pocket, rolled it between his fingers, and bit off the end. He lit it up and leaned against the helicopter, studying Catherine as she approached.

"What can I do for you, Ms. Celeste?" he said with a crisp English accent.

"Bobby," Celeste replied, "I'd like you to meet Catherine Lloyd."

Bobby nodded. "How do you do, Ms. Lloyd?"

"I'm well."

Catherine shook his hand. It was rough like sandpaper.

"Catherine could use a lift back to Monrovia. Do you think you could accommodate her?"

"It would be my pleasure."

Mama, I'm coming for you.

Bobby and Celeste walked off to talk terms.

Catherine turned to Benjamin and took his hands between hers. "I will tell Mama that you are well." He nodded and took hold of the carry-on and placed the valise under his arm. He carried them to the door of the helicopter and placed the carry-on inside.

When Bobby and Celeste returned, Celeste looked a little troubled.

"Is everything OK?" Catherine asked.

"Yes, of course," Celeste replied, recovering her smile.

"Well, I guess this is it," she added and hugged Catherine tightly. Catherine felt the baby kick.

"I guess your little one is telling us to get on with it," Catherine said with a smile.

Benjamin handed the valise to Catherine. "Is there something you want to leave with me, Ms. Catherine?"

She opened the valise and handed him the brown bag containing her gun. "Thank you for reminding me."

Benjamin smiled.

Bobby helped Catherine into the helicopter.

"Welcome aboard."

He pinched the end of his cigar and put it in his breast pocket.

"Take care, Ms. Celeste. In case anyone else is looking for a lift to Liberia, I'll be back in a week."

Bobby climbed in and closed the door.

"Ever rode in a 'copter, Ms. Catherine?" he said, putting on a headset to drown out the noise and handing one to Catherine as well.

"No. This is my first time."

Bobby flipped switches on the dashboard. "Well, hold on," he yelled over the noise of the helicopter gearing up. "It's a bit choppy, but this bird is as smooth as they come. Most people take short trips, twenty or thirty minutes. It's about as much as they can handle. The one you're taking lasts a couple hours. We'll have to make a stop at Lungi Island for petro first."

Catherine took hold of a strap hanging from the ceiling of the cabin and waved good-bye as the helicopter began to lift off.

God bless you, Bobby Latimore.

The ride was uneventful until they arrived at Robertsfield Airport. A group of Liberian soldiers ran out of a building and rushed toward the helicopter as it landed. Bobby looked in their direction with mild interest, but tension gripped Catherine's back and shoulder. The nine soldiers held AK-47 semiautomatic rifles. Catherine wished she had held on to the handgun.

Three of the soldiers wore wigs and bras over their undershirts. A soldier in full uniform, including boots and sunglasses, brought up the rear. He pushed his way through them, then banged on the helicopter door impatiently.

Unconcerned, Bobby continued shutting down the aircraft.

"How was the ride?"

"I can't think of any other that was worse."

Bobby laughed and took off his seat belt. "May I have your papers, Ms. Catherine? These blokes will want to see them."

Catherine took out her passport and the letter bearing Claypool Mensa's signature. Bobby looked them over, reached in his pocket, took out six bills—sixty American dollars—and folded them inside the letter. He took the cigar stub out of his pocket and clenched it between his teeth. "This shouldn't take long."

Bobby got out. The soldiers crowded around him. Their eyes were bloodshot. Their expressions were brooding. Reluctantly, they made room for him to pass. Bobby approached the leader and handed him the documents. He took them with barely a glance. He flipped through the passport and handed it back. Then he unfolded the letter and tucked the money in his breast pocket without counting it. After reading the letter, he looked in Catherine's direction and returned it to Bobby. He said something. Bobby frowned. Clearly unhappy, the leader turned and walked away. Bobby watched him for a moment, chewing on his cigar. Finally, he said something that made the soldier stop short, turn around, and walk back. The cigar in Bobby's mouth bobbed up and down while the leader pointed his finger at Bobby's nose and yelled. Bobby reached into his pocket and peeled off three more bills.

Suddenly the door to the helicopter flew open. A soldier wearing a blond wig peered into the cabin. His eyes fell immediately on the valise.

"Is there something I can help you with?" Catherine said, thinking about the money inside.

Another soldier came up behind the first.

The first soldier looked past Catherine at the instruments on the dashboard and at the purse on her lap. He stretched his neck to see what else was in the helicopter.

"Where are you from?" Catherine asked, hoping to distract him.

He seemed puzzled by the question. He recovered after a moment and reached for the valise.

"Don't touch that," Catherine said sharply. He smirked. "I don't see anyone big enough here to stop me," he mumbled in Mende.

"It is not the size of the genitals that matters, it is the size of the heart," responded Catherine likewise in Mende.

"You know my language?" the soldier said in surprise. "Yes," said Catherine. "I have met many people from your tribe."

Bobby came back to the helicopter and climbed in the other side. "Your lieutenant wants to talk to you." The soldiers exchanged looks and closed the door.

"Are you all right?" Bobby asked, scanning Catherine's face.

Catherine breathed a sigh of relief. "I'm fine."

Bobby glanced down at her leg. It was shaking. She put her hand on it to steady herself.

"So what do we do now?"

"We wait until my friend arrives."

"How long will that take?"

"Maybe a half hour or less."

Bobby lit his cigar, puffed, and blew smoke rings. He glanced over at Catherine and said, "You don't remember me, do you?"

"I don't believe we've met before. I think I would remember you."

"Well, we didn't meet formally. I was at the embassy when the marines brought you back from the Ducor Hotel."

"Really?"

"It was my lucky day," Bobby chuckled wryly. "A batch of medicine for a clinic in the bush arrived that day, and I was there to pick it up and deliver it. Bloody hell broke out while I was waiting."

Catherine stared at Bobby for a moment, then leaned back in the seat.

"I hope I didn't upset you," Bobby said.

She cleared her throat but did not answer him.

An old jeep pulled up in front of the helicopter. A black priest with salt-and-pepper hair got out and waved.

"Here's our ride."

Father Michael ran an orphanage twenty miles outside Monrovia. It was one of a few orphanages still operating.

"Father Michael takes care of me when I'm in the area," Bobby said after they were on the road for a few minutes.

"We're not going to make it to Monrovia before sundown," said Father Michael. He had an African accent. "I would suggest that you stay at the orphanage tonight. The accommodations are very modest, Ms. Catherine. Isn't that so, Bobby?" The priest chuckled.

Bobby grinned. "They're OK, Father Michael," he replied.

Night had fallen when they turned onto the road that cut through the bush to the orphanage. Father Michael's familiarity with how and when the road would bend was the only insurance that the car would not fall into the ditches alongside. It was a bumpy ride. A fragrant branch from a bush reached into the car and gently brushed Catherine's cheek. *Mama is close now,* Catherine thought as her hand sought out the locket and closed around it.

"Here we are," Father Michael said. They pulled up to the parsonage, a small house made of stone with a screened-in porch. The orphanage had five small houses and two tents—one for schooling; the other for medical emergencies; two cabins for the staff, one for the men and the other for the women—and seven moderately sized houses where the children slept. The staff had dwindled to eight volunteers and some local women who slept with the orphans at night. Sixty-seven children lived at the orphanage. There was an open area where large pots sat on charred coals, picnic tables, and benches. A matronly woman opened the door and came out.

"How are you this evening, Mama?" Bobby said.

"I am very well, Bobby," the woman responded.

"Ms. Catherine, I would like to introduce you to Tantee Daisy," Father Michael said. "Tantee Daisy is a missionary in Côte d'Ivoire, and she has come to help me train the new volunteers. She is going back to Sierra Leone with Bobby, and then she's going home to the States."

"Good evening," said Tantee Daisy. Her eyes twinkled. Her close-cropped soft curly hair was streaked with random strands of gray. She spoke with an Africana French accent.

"I am happy to make your acquaintance," Catherine said in French.

"Oh, you speak French!" Tantee Daisy exclaimed in Francofone French. Her enthusiasm was infectious. "Welcome to Saint Therese Orphanage."

Catherine and Daisy continued to converse in French as they went into the house. Catherine learned that Daisy had grown up in Philadelphia and had been in the mission field in Côte d'Ivoire for twenty years. Her brother named Joseph lived in Fairmount, just around the corner from Catherine.

Coincidence? No confirmation. This is where I am supposed to be.

"Catherine and Bobby will be staying with us this evening," Father Michael told Daisy.

"I hope you're hungry," she replied. "The supplies came in today, and the soldiers actually left something for the orphanage this time."

The staff, all in their twenties and Caucasian except for one African American woman, was curious about the young woman Bobby was traveling with. They exchanged looks with one another when he held Catherine's chair. It was a side of him they have never seen.

After dinner, Bobby, Catherine, Father Michael, and Daisy went out to the porch and talked about the state of affairs in Liberia with the volunteers.

"This is a good discussion, but I'm sorry I will have to retire," Father Michael said after an hour and a half of conversation and speculation about the peacekeeping troops. "What is happening is good, but we need medication. Fortunately, there are no sick children to take care of this evening. This is the first time in many weeks that we are all able to go to bed at the same time."

"I think Father Michael is suggesting that we should all go to bed now," Daisy said, raising.

Dutifully, the volunteers stood and said good night. They turned on their flashlights and headed for the cabins, still talking about the day's events.

The night was filled with the sound of crickets. Hundreds of fireflies drifted lazily and aimlessly in the darkness. Bobby sat on a straight-back chair. He lit up a cigar. Pensive, Catherine sat in a rocker.

"How are you doing, Ms. Catherine?"

"I'm fine, Bobby, and you?" she replied, rocking gently, gazing at the pattern of on-and-off light the fireflies were making.

"I'm happy to be alive," he responded, puffing on the cigar.

Catherine looked up at the moon. After several minutes, she said, "There's something I want to ask you, Bobby."

"What is it?"

"Would you tell me what I was like when they brought me back to the embassy that night?"

Bobby took the cigar out of his mouth.

"Why do you want to dredge up that old stuff?"

"There are things I don't quite remember, and everyone who was there that night is so tight-lipped there's no point trying to talk to them about it. I need to know about my state of mind."

"Why is that important to you?"

"I don't know. Sometimes I have dreams and . . ." Catherine frowned. "Never mind."

"Would you like to know what I think?"

"About what?" Catherine stared at Bobby blankly.

"About talking about the past."

"You don't care for it."

"Actually, I don't mind at all. But I don't think you're interested in how you appeared that night. I think you want something else. If I was in your shoes, I would want to tell my story to anyone who would be willing to listen because it's good for the soul. I've had my share of opportunities to get things off my chest. Bars are good places for that sort of thing. Complete strangers are sometimes the best listeners. They don't have to get involved. They may not be your family or friends, but it gets the job done. I can honestly say that I'm all the better for having done it."

Bobby tilted his chair back against the wall and blew two perfectly round smoke rings into the air. Catherine watched them drift, expand, and dissolve.

"I've gotten on with my life since the coup," she began slowly. "I've even gone for months without having a single thought about it, but eventually it all comes back."

"That's what we do. We keep moving until it catches up with us."

Catherine took a deep breath.

"It was my last year in school," she began. "My friends were named Olivia, Joy, Bennet, and Luis. They were my best friends, and it was their last year too. We went to the Ducor to have dinner and talk about our parties. We were planning to go to the clubs on Broad Street after dinner. It was the first time we had gone out without chaperons."

Catherine paused. Remembering was like sifting through the ashes of a fire.

"My father was in Washington. I don't know why I didn't tell anyone where I was going. I was supposed to. That was the agreement. I was so excited I guess I forgot. I remembered later, but by that time, we had already been out for two hours and it didn't seem like such a big deal. Besides, everyone knew everyone else in Monrovia. I wasn't concerned."

Catherine stopped and looked down at her hands.

"Go on, Ms. Catherine," Bobby encouraged.

"I should have seen it coming, Bobby," she continued. "It was always there, the jealousy, I mean. I'd overheard the things my friend's servants used to say behind their backs. Some of it was true. They did spend too much money all the time on everything. All the Americo-Liberian children were spoiled in ways my father never would have allowed. I guess I just accepted it as the way things were. The white children were just as spoiled. Well, maybe not all of them."

"I know all about that, Ms. Catherine," Bobby said. "Remember I'm British. We colonized Africa and gave Africa a model for how to be the ruling class. Never should have been here in the first place. The Americo-Liberian families did what every ruling class does—live like kings and queens. They made all the mistakes of the privileged. You know how it goes. The poor rise up and kill the rich. In Europe, we call it revolution."

Catherine began to rock slowly.

"We were having such a good time until the soldiers came into the dining room. The first lot was drunk silly. They were laughing and falling down. But then others arrived, and they were sober. Everything happened so fast. We didn't have time to think."

Catherine stood up and began to pace. She stopped. Her eyes were wide, as though she was watching a scene far-off. She halted, then began again.

"They went from one table to the other, taking whatever they wanted, shoving food into their mouths, spilling beer on the floor, down the front of their shirts and on people. The way they were acting seemed deliberate to me, like they were trying to make a point. We started looking at each other, wondering what was going on. These boys never came to the Ducor without the generals. I think a couple of people left the room to look for the manager, but I'm not sure. They didn't come back."

Catherine leaned against the doorframe. After a moment, she sat back down in the chair and started rocking, this time a little faster.

"I had a crush on Bennet. He was stronger than the rest of us. At first I was glad he was there, but then things got crazy between him and the soldiers. He kept an eye on them while the rest of us talked. I remember Luis saying, 'Can you believe this?' Joy kept asking, 'What are they doing here?' as if one of us could explain it to her. Bennet was getting angrier by the second. It wasn't as if this was the first time we had seen soldiers drink. They always got drunk on payday. We thought that maybe that was it. They finally had a little money so . . ."

Catherine stopped. "I'm not sure I have the sequence right, Bobby."

Bobby leaned forward, searching Catherine's face. "Not important, Ms. Catherine."

"I remember saying, 'Maybe we should leave,' or something like that. Yes, I'm sure that's what I said."

Catherine rubbed her forehead as if to ease something from her mind, or possibly relieve the tension that arises when a person is caught between fighting to remember and wishing to forget. "Are you all right? Can I get you some water or something?" Bobby asked, nervous.

Catherine smiled weakly. "Is this too much for you?"

"I was wondering the same thing about you," Bobby responded, wishing he'd had a drink.

"It's always been too much."

Silence.

"We were about to leave when more soldiers came in. A couple of them stood by the door while the others started walking around the room, giving people dirty looks. I started to feel nervous. I was sure the police would come. I kept looking at the door but . . ." Catherine's voice drifted. "Bennet went over to a group of them. I followed him. They were his friends—at least I thought they were. Bennet told them they couldn't come into the dining room, and the boys started to laugh. One of them said, 'Fuck you, Bennet. We can do whatever we want to do now.' 'Fuck me?' Bennet yelled back at him. I'd never seen him so angry. The soldier swore at him again. His friends made a circle around Bennet. Bennet and the boy stood there, staring each other down. Then the boy pushed Bennet and he fell down, and his friends pointed their guns at him.

"'Your President Tolbout is dead, Bennet, dead! Sergeant Doe shot him,' the boy who shoved Bennet said. We were all stunned. Bennet stared up at him in disbelief. The president was his uncle. The soldier stood over Bennet, laughing and shaking his finger. 'You're going to get yours too,' he said, and then he and his friends left. Bennet got up and came back to the table. His eyes were filled with tears. I was stunned. The dining room was buzzing. Some people burst into tears. Everyone was getting up to leave, but the soldiers blocked the door. We heard shouting and cries coming from the lobby. It sounded like things were being thrown around. I was so scared I couldn't think. Olivia was hysterical. She kept saying over and over, 'They're not going to let us out. They're going to keep us here.' Joy and I started crying. I took her hand, and she whispered, 'I want to go home now. Please, please, can we go home now?' I told her that things were going to be all right. I didn't know what else to say."

Catherine stopped and took a deep breath, her expression pained. She turned to Bobby. "When I finish getting this out, I'm going to be OK, right?"

"Go on, Ms. Catherine."

There was compassion in his voice.

Catherine looked up at the moon and sighed.

"This is harder than I thought it would be."

"Just stay with it as long as you like. You're doing better than I did the first time I talked about my demons," Bobby said. "It took a couple of tries.

I trashed my apartment one of those times. Knocked a whole in the wall. I drank to kill the pain."

"Mama helped me deal with my pain."

"You're lucky."

Silence.

"I don't know what made me notice the elderly couple a few tables away except that they were acting as if nothing was going on," Catherine continued. "When the man stood up and held her chair so calmly, something went through me. She was very old and very frail. They didn't get far because a soldier ran over to them and started shouting obscenities. I'd never seen elders treated this way. Before I knew it, I was on my feet going after him. Olivia caught my arm, and Luis and Bennet came around and stood in front of me. The soldier hit the old man, and I started crying again. Bennet grabbed me and held me while I cried. Luis patted my back. Then the soldiers made everyone stand up and move to one side of the dining room. There were about fifty people there.

They started letting people go until the only people left were me and the Americo-Liberians. They made the men give them their wallets and watches and took the women's purses and jewelry. Joy took off her earrings and slipped them to me. She whispered to me to take her earrings. They belonged to her mother. She said, 'if these boys get hold of them, I'll never see them again, and my mother will be so upset with me.' The others must have heard her because Olivia took off her brooch and handed it to me behind her back. Bennet and Luis took off their watches and slipped them to me. I remember their faces, their sadness and fear. Their jewelry felt so cold. Do you think they knew they were going to die?"

"Maybe," Bobby said. "I think people sense when their time is just about up."

Silence.

"I sometimes think that if I had put up more resistance when the soldier told me to leave, things would have turned out different."

"Don't second-guess yourself, Catherine. You were a kid. These boys were not to be played with. Didn't the marines find you locked in a room?"

"Bennet asked one of the soldiers he had been friendly with to help me. He and another soldier locked me in a room instead."

Catherine's eyes filled up with tears. "Sometimes I still can't believe it happened the way I remember it. It's like a bad dream," she whispered, wiping away tears. She stood and began pacing.

"All I kept thinking about was how my friends and I were going to get away. I didn't know where the soldiers had taken them, but I thought I could find them and we could escape together. I tried the door but it was locked, so I used a bobby pin and tried to jimmy it like they do in the movies but that didn't work. I called the embassy after that, but the lines were all busy. I was so frustrated that I sat down on the floor and started crying. But I made myself stop."

Catherine turned to Bobby. "I don't know how I did that. I was so scared."

"We are able to do unusual things under extreme stress," Bobby said. "We really don't know our own strength until then."

"I thought I could get out of the room through the window, so I took the sheets off the bed and started tying the ends together and praying that no one would catch me climbing out. The soldiers were running up and down the halls, shouting and shooting off their guns. I hoped they would keep at it because as long as they were busy, they wouldn't be interested in me or what I might be doing . . ."

Catherine's expression glazed over. "It was the first time in my life that there was no one around to watch over me." Tears formed in her eyes, and her bottom lip quivered. She sniffed, then came back to the chair. "I said the Lord's Prayer while I pushed the bed close to the window and tied one end of the sheets around the leg of the bed and tossed the other end out the window. It didn't go very far. I thought I would probably sprain my ankle when I dropped, but I really didn't care. I kept thinking about Josh, one of the soccer players at school who played a game with a sprain and Tylenol. I imagined being him, playing through the pain. I was trying to figure out the best way to climb down when the soldier, the one Bennett had asked to help me, opened the door."

Catherine stopped.

"What happened, Ms. Catherine?" Bobby asked gently.

Silence.

"You don't have to talk about that part if you don't want to," Bobby said.

"I know what you're thinking," Catherine responded slowly, "but he didn't rape me. He would have to kill me first. He tore my blouse off, but I brought my knee up so hard between his legs that I swear I heard something crack. He doubled over in pain, and that ended that. He pushed me, left the room, and locked the door again."

"I heard something, so I went back to the window and I saw my friends. The soldiers were walking behind them drinking beer. The moon was very bright that night. Olivia had her arm around Joy's shoulder. Luis and Bennet were walking behind them. I called to them and they stopped and looked up, but the soldiers pushed them and shouted at them to keep moving and . . .'"

Catherine paused, unable to catch her breath. She stood up and doubled over. Bobby sprang to his feet and started toward her. She held up one hand. "It's OK, Bobby," she managed. She forced herself upright.

"I could see everything. The waves were high . . ." Catherine wrapped her arms around her body as if she was cold. "Then they stopped, and the soldiers lined them up and shot them. I heard a scream before they fell down. It shot through my head like a bullet. The soldiers walked away, drinking beer and laughing."

Catherine began to pace again. Tears streamed down her face.

"All of the feeling left me. I couldn't feel anything, not my hands or my legs. There was a ringing in my head. Then I thought I saw them move, so I started yelling, 'Get up! Get up! Please get up! I'm coming!' I remembered putting one foot up on the windowsill and getting ready to jump. It felt like someone else was getting ready to jump. I couldn't quite feel my body. I heard Olivia say, 'Walk away, Catherine. Do not look at us.' It sounded like she was standing right behind me. Then Bennet said, 'Go back in the room. Take care of yourself. Calm yourself. There is nothing you can do for us now.' I brought my legs back over the windowsill, and that's the last thing I remembered before waking up in the hospital."

Catherine sat back in the chair. Bobby handed her his handkerchief. She wiped her eyes.

"Thank you," Catherine said. She took a deep breath. "I have dreams where I wake up while I'm being carried out of the Ducor by the marines and there's fire all around me. There's another dream where a man is being chased down the street by a mob."

"People were pretty shook up when they saw the condition you were in. Your father's secretary started crying."

"I think she blamed herself for what happened." Catherine sighed. "It wasn't her fault."

"You're a brave young woman, Ms. Catherine," Bobby said.

"Thank you, Bobby," Catherine replied. "But I don't think its bravery. Since the coup, I think about death a great deal. If I don't act, I believe I will die. I survived the coup for a reason. I haven't figured that part out yet, but I will."

Catherine stood. Bobby handed her a flashlight and opened the porch door.

"Sleep well, Ms. Catherine."

CHAPTER NINETEEN

April 17
The Road to Monrovia

Catherine was pouring a cup of coffee when Bobby walked in the kitchen. She looked at him and smiled gently. Her hair was wet and slicked back from her face, glistening. Earlier, she had bathed in a river that Tantee Daisy had pointed the way to.

"Good morning. Coffee?" she said, holding up the pot.

"Yes, please. You're up early."

The grandfather clock in the living room chimed seven times.

"The phones are working," Catherine said, handing Bobby a cup. "I woke Claypool up."

"How is the old boy?"

"Surprised that I'm in Liberia. I told him that you brought me. He's expecting us later this morning."

"We should leave in the next hour if we're going to keep that date."

"We can leave sooner than that," Catherine said. "I'm already packed,"

When Catherine and Bobby had finished loading up the jeep, Father Michael took Bobby aside to talk to him in private. Tantee Daisy stayed with Catherine. "Watch out for rebels. They're popping up everywhere now," she warned. She held Catherine's hands and prayed for a safe journey, while Bobby kneeled and Father Michael made the sign of the cross on his forehead.

Like all the roads in West Africa, the road to Monrovia was rough and bumpy. But unlike those close to villages, it was also barren. The absence of village women walking from one place to another with large bundles of clothes, or baskets filled with fruit and other things on their heads, and men holding up bush meat for sale disturbed Catherine. In the silence, she sensed the crimes against the villagers. Bobby glanced over at her and saw that she was deep in thought.

At the first checkpoint, Senegalese soldiers smartly dressed in pressed military uniforms flirted with Catherine once they established that she had hitched a ride with Bobby and was not his woman. Although Catherine's manner was curt and aloof, they persisted in asking routine questions about inane matters. Their interest was not dampened even after she put on her sunglasses. In fact, her attempt to ignore them had the opposite effect. Angered, she slipped and replied to one of their questions in rapid-fire French. Finally, an officer pulled up and finished the job and passed them though. What should have only taken five minutes had taken thirty.

"What a crock of shit," Catherine fumed.

After a moment, she calmed down and smiled.

"Why are you smiling?" Bobby asked, curious.

"They did me a favor. I needed the distraction. I'm OK now."

"Splendid."

As they approached the second checkpoint, Catherine noticed something hanging in a tree.

"What is that?" She pointed at a scarecrow hanging from a rope, dressed in fatigues, a bandana, hat, and army shirt.

Bobby squinted. "Oh Christ," he exclaimed.

Catherine gasped. "Stop the car!"

The scarecrow was the skeletal remains of what appeared to be a child who had not been more than seven years old. Horror swept through Catherine like electricity. She turned her head, shielded her eyes, and took a deep breath. A hundred feet away, Liberian soldiers gathered at the roadblock and stood watching them.

"Just give me a moment." Catherine lowered her trembling hand. She forced herself to look at the child's remains. She removed the pendant holding Madame Chief's picture and put it in her pocket. "OK, Bobby. I'm ready."

A soldier stepped onto the road and put up his hand. Bobby stopped the jeep and waited as he approached. "Your papers please," he said roughly. Bobby handed him his and Catherine's passports along with Catherine's travel papers. The other soldiers circled the jeep. They watched Bobby with stolid red-veined eyes. Bobby casually threw his arm over the back of the seat. Catherine put her sunglasses on. Lacking any true interest in the routine, the soldiers walked away, passing a bottle of whiskey between them. Bobby spotted another soldier approaching the jeep from the rear. He held a gun with both hands. The barrel was pointed at the ground, but his eyes were trained on the back of Bobby's head.

"There's one coming up on your side. Don't let him rattle you."

The soldier examining Catherine's travel papers waved the advancing soldier away from the car.

A child soldier barely twelve years old emerged from the bush, zipping his fly. He walked up to the other soldiers and started making grunting sounds. They ignored him. He stopped, turned toward Catherine, and mumbled. He raised his pointer finger cocked around the trigger of an imaginary gun and aimed at her. His intent was clear. Catherine braced herself as the boy shot her three times. The soldier questioning Bobby stopped and yelled to the boy to go away. The boy scowled and walked a few feet away. He stopped, turned to Catherine, and stared. His eyes bulged. He grimaced. He grabbed his head with both hands as if it hurt. Calmer, Catherine watched him, feeling compassion. She asked God to help him.

"You may go," the soldier said. His eyes followed the jeep some distance as Bobby and Catherine drove away.

They drove in silence. Catherine closed her eyes and whispered the Lord's Prayer. She kept them closed while the wind brushed her face. She heard birds singing. She thought about the series of events that had pushed her toward Monrovia. She thought about Marcus and yearned to see him, to talk to him. She imagined sitting with him in his apartment, recounting everything. She pictured him sitting in his leather recliner, listening attentively as she told him about the encounter with the Liberian soldiers. She imagined him nodding in agreement with her views on the situation in Liberia. Finally, Catherine thought about how she would apologize for the worry she'd caused him.

She opened her eyes and looked around.

"How long before the next checkpoint?"

"It's hard to say, Ms. Catherine. Maybe five miles."

The next stretch of road was littered with small potholes. Jostled about, Catherine grabbed hold of the doorframe.

"How are we doing?" Bobby asked.

"I hope the axle doesn't break."

This time, they drove farther than ten miles. All the roadblocks had not been set up yet. They passed a group of soldiers who had captured six rebels. The rebels were sitting on the ground with their hands behind their heads. Dust covered their hair, arms, legs, shirts, and pants. One rebel looked into Catherine's eyes as they passed. His face was full of anger and rage. She held his gaze and felt nothing.

"The next checkpoint will probably be the last between here and Monrovia," Bobby commented as they spotted one up the road.

As they neared the checkpoint, Catherine noted with relief that there was a bustle of life around it. About fifty feet away from the road, four jeeps and a Red Cross truck were parked outside a shack that had been turned into a field office. Directly behind it was a small village. The shacks were barely standing, held up with old gray boards and rusting scrap metal. A few had paltry gardens on the side, home to leggy tomato bushes with wrinkled sunburned leaves. A goat was tied to a pole stuck in the ground. Children with dusty bare feet ran near the houses, carefree. Two women walked by holding baskets of wash on their hips. Young men, their faces worn by too many brushes with rebels and death, sat side by side on chairs strung along a wall. One was missing an arm, another both legs. They watched the soldiers and talked to one another.

Catherine noticed a woman sitting on a chair in a doorway, holding a sleeping child, and staring into space. A dingy kerchief was tied around her head. The flowers on her dress had faded. Her features were chiseled and expressionless. She looked frozen, removed from the life of the village around her. Catherine wondered about the child sleeping contently in her lap. Naked, the child was round and cherub-like. It did not seem possible that it belonged to the woman.

That's what I must have looked like when I was ill.

"Good morning, sir," a soldier said politely.

A Ghanian, he was dressed in a regular army uniform.

"Good morning," Bobby replied and handed him the papers.

The soldier studied the documents, glanced at Catherine, then walked over to where his comrades were standing at a makeshift gate, a rope strung across the road tied to two trees on opposite sides. They gathered around as he showed them Catherine's passport.

"What's going on?"

"I don't know."

The soldier headed for the office.

"I hope he doesn't take too long."

The sun was directly overhead. Catherine took off her hat and fanned her face with it. Several minutes passed. The door of the office opened, and a man dressed in a sergeant's uniform came out. His stomach hung over his belt, and he breathed heavily as he lumbered toward the jeep. The soldier who had delivered Catherine's passport walked behind him, eclipsed by the sergeant's girth.

"Good afternoon, Ms. Lloyd," the sergeant said.

"Good afternoon," said Catherine. "Is there a problem with my passport?"

"No. Your papers are fine." He handed the documents to Bobby. "I have a message from your father."

"My father?"

"Yes. We have been on the lookout for you all morning."

"How did my father know I was coming this way?"

Bobby cleared his throat. "I believe Celeste contacted him. She said she would as soon as the lines were working."

"I see," Catherine replied, glad that someone had let Marcus know where she was, and grateful that her ties to him were operating as effectively as they always had. Now she would not have to think about contacting him and explaining.

"What is the message?" she said.

"Your father would like you to stop at the Mamba Point Hotel. A letter is waiting there for you."

Monrovia

The faces of some of the city's landmarks had been torn away by bomb blasts. Stagnant pools of water, breeding grounds for mosquitoes carrying malaria, lay in the alleys. Locals casually walked in front of boxy white UN vehicles with three-feet-high logos, soldier-driven jeeps, and Red Cross vans. Catherine looked around as if she was seeing the city of Monrovia for the first time.

The pictures and films Catherine had seen on the six o'clock news had barely prepared her for a city in limbo, waiting to be rescued from a vicious cycle of one war after another. There had been two since the last time Catherine was there.

They traveled down Broad Street and stopped at the corner. The traffic had stalled at the intersection. They waited. The door to a store, its windows boarded up, opened. Catherine looked inside and saw the owners, a man and his wife, and remembered them. The man wore a *kufee* and the woman wore a veil. The man was handing a customer his purchase, which was wrapped in newspaper. The woman was folding what looked like baby clothes. There were only a few items for sale on the shelves—peanuts in recycled wine bottles, flip-flops, a few canned goods, bandages, alcohol, and other random items. The merchandise was spaced far apart, as though the empty places were reserved for goods on backorder. The man looked out and noticed Catherine. He waved. She waved back. She wondered if he recognized her or if he was just being friendly. Not that it mattered. At that moment, Catherine was desperately longing for something ordinary and familiar, a sign that life had continued in spite of the war. His gesture gave her hope.

When they reached the Mamba Point Hotel, Claypool Mensa was sitting in a chair outside the door. He raised his arms and welcomed her.

"My sister!"

"Double O!"

Claypool kissed Catherine on both cheeks. "You have not changed, except for the company you are keeping these days." He chortled and slapped Bobby on the shoulder. "I trust there was no trouble getting through the roadblocks," he added, suddenly serious.

"I'd say we made fairly good time," Bobby replied.

"Thank you for the travel papers, Claypool," Catherine said. "You saved me a great deal of trouble."

"Good, very good," Claypool smiled once again.

"You look well. How are your parents and your sisters and brothers?" Catherine asked.

"They are all well. My sister Tata was very excited when I told her you were coming to Monrovia. She is married now and has three children."

"And you? Do you have a wife?"

"Of course. I have two children, with one on the way." He made a circle out from his body with his arms. "Any day now. And you, are you married?"

"No."

"This is too hard to believe. Been waiting for the right fellow?"

"Yes." Clifton flashed through Catherine's mind. It felt strange to think of him. It seemed as if she had known him in another life.

Claypool reached into the breast pocket of his military shirt. "I have something for you. It is a letter from your father. He dictated it over the phone to my secretary."

"Is there any news about Mama?"

"We are pretty certain we know where she is. Read your father's letter, and then we will talk. Come, sit here." Claypool brushed off the chair he'd been sitting in. "Have you had lunch?" he asked Bobby as both men walked off toward the jeep.

> Dear Catherine:
>
> Please do not be discouraged. I will continue my efforts as will others.
>
> Thank Robert Latimore for me and give Claypool Mensa my regards.
>
> Call me when you are settled.
>
> Marcus

I'll call when it's over, Daddy. Catherine sighed, put the letter in her pocket, then hurried to catch up with Claypool and Bobby.

Claypool's hangout was a block away, the Mandarin Chinese restaurant.

It was exactly as Catherine had remembered it. Somehow it had survived intact. The lobby was painted red, and a dragon was painted on the wall behind the receptionist counter. The owner Sam Lin Phat's long mustache and beard were now white, and he was blind. He still wore traditional Chinese clothes. He sat in a corner smiling while his son, Chou, handled the customers.

Chou showed them to one of the booths "reserved for the big shots."

The restaurant was bustling with customers: ECOMOG troops, Nigerian generals, bush pilots, petty entrepreneurs, diamond smugglers, spies, and members of Liberia's underworld. The room had small windows and Chinese lanterns, but it was still extremely dim. The air in the room was thick and stale.

The waiter came over to take their orders. Bobby polished off a beer and stood up to leave.

"I have to get petro. There's no telling how long it will take to find some with so many military vehicles about." Claypool told him where he could find some. Bobby signaled the waiter. After paying the bill, he turned to Catherine. "I guess you're OK now?"

"Yes," she said.

"What do you think, my brother? She's with me now," Claypool said, flashing a big smile.

Catherine watched Bobby leave the restaurant.

Silence.

Claypool looked around the room and then at Catherine. Neither one smiled.

"What do you want to do?"

"Nothing has changed."

Catherine had asked Claypool to help her find mercenaries when she spoke to him that morning.

"Very well. There is one officer who I think you can trust to do the job. His name is Colonel Craig Olatungi. He is one of Nigeria's best."

"Where did he get his formal military training?" Catherine asked.

"He attended Sandhurst Military Academy in the UK. He is a most capable officer, and he has done wet work in the past. I will do the negotiating for you."

Catherine was relieved to hear that Col. Olatungi had attended Sandhurst Military Academy, the West Point of the UK. It meant that he was a professional soldier and that he would handpick his men. She was a little curious about how much wet work—covert operations sponsored by the CIA—he had done, but her curiosity was overshadowed by a greater need.

"You can negotiate the contract, but I want to meet him."

Claypool's eyebrows shot up. "I doubt that he will agree to that. You know that is not the way it is done. This man is not interested in his benefactor."

"I want to look into the eyes of the man who I am trusting to bring Mama home safely. He needs to look into my eyes to see that this is more than business as usual."

"Are you not listening, woman?" Claypool bristled with an angry glint in his eyes.

"Col. Olatungi is not someone you can bargain with about these things!"

"How much will this cost me?" Catherine shot back, unmoved by Claypool's agitation.

"For what?"

"For you to arrange this meeting."

Claypool paused. "I am not doing this for the money."

"How much, Claypool?"

"I can see that you are determined," he said, smiling with everything but his eyes. "I cannot give you any assurances."

"Claypool, if you do this for me, I will always be indebted to you. Now . . . will five hundred American do?"

"I will see what I can do. We will discuss the money later."

Catherine was concerned that she had offended Claypool and damaged their relationship. She decided to let the matter of payment for the additional favor drop and to not bring it up again no matter what happened.

*   *   *

Dressed in an officer's uniform, complete with insignias, medals, and hat, Col. Olatungi eyed Catherine coolly as she sat down opposite him. He wore opaque sunglasses. She saw just enough of his eyes to know they were stern and guarded. He was younger than she had imaged he would be. His men stood nearby at attention.

It was 4:00 p.m. The Palm Hotel was a family vacation hotel gone to seed. Her memories of the Palm gathered around her like friendly spirits as she sat waiting for Col. Olatungi to speak.

"Why have you come to me?" he asked.

"I want the best, and I've been told that you have been trained for this type of job," Catherine replied.

"And . . ."

"I wanted to see the man I am counting on."

"This job will cost fifteen thousand for me and eight thousand for each of my best men," Col. Olatungi responded a little impatiently. "I will bring ten of them. I will also bring six others, good men. They will cost you three thousand each, American."

Catherine sensed that the colonel thought the figures would put her off. Knowing she was several thousand dollars short, she decided to call his bluff anyway.

"That is acceptable. When will you go?"

She felt his eyes coolly peruse her face.

"We will leave before sunrise tomorrow. The entire job should be over very quickly, and we will have Madame Chief back here before noon."

"I want to go with you."

Col. Olatungi's eyes hardened.

"No. This is a contract. I never take women on my jobs."

"Why not?"

"It is not done."

"I will stay out of your way, as far back as you would like until you send for me. Assign a man to me, and I will pay double your price."

"This is not how I do my business."

"I am aware of that."

His eyes scanned her face, and this time her body as well. Catherine steeled herself under his scrutiny.

"Claypool tells me that you came from America to do this. Is that right?"

"Yes."

"Who is Madame Chief to you?"

"She is my Mama."

"How did she become your Mama?"

"What does that matter?"

"It doesn't."

Col. Olatungi leaned back and eyed Catherine coolly and deliberately. Catherine felt sweat rolling down the back of her neck, but she forced herself to match his stare.

"I look into your eyes, and I see something I have not seen before," he said. "But my word is final."

He stood up and left the hotel, his men in tow.

*   *   *

Catherine took a room at the Mamba Point Hotel.

There was a knock at the door.

Startled out of sleep, she sat up quickly.

"Who is it?"

"Sorry to wake you, madame, but I have a message from Col. Olatungi."

Catherine checked her watch. It was four in the morning. She cracked the door open and saw a soldier.

"Yes."

"Col. Olatungi has sent me to tell you that you may go."

CHAPTER TWENTY

April 18, 5:00 a.m.
The Rescue

Bobby was waiting at the rendezvous point when she arrived.

"How did you find out about this?" Catherine asked.

"Claypool called me. Col. Olatungi and I are old friends. I've flown his plane a few times. He's an unusual sort. No predicting him. I would have bet against this," Bobby said, referring to the colonel's decision to let Catherine tag along. "I had to come down here to see for myself . . . and to check on you."

"You're a good man, Bobby," Catherine offered. "I will understand if you decide to alert our embassy about this," Catherine said.

"I am confident that Col. Olatungi will get the job done," Bobby replied.

"I know this road, Bobby. If anything unexpected happens . . ."

"Trust me. They won't know what hit them."

In the back of Catherine's mind, she feared that the rescue mission could go badly. She looked around at the men—dressed in fatigues, boots, and the black caps of professional soldiers—the trucks, the jeeps, and the colonel. This was her last chance to stop it. She could not. She hoped Bobby was right.

"Take care, Ms. Catherine," Bobby said and opened the car door. It was much heavier than normal. The tires were also larger and thicker. Catherine knew immediately it was a bulletproof car.

When the soldier assigned to drive for her turned the key in the ignition, Catherine's pulse quickened. *No turning around now.* Hers was the last vehicle to pull onto the road.

∗   ∗   ∗

7:00 a.m.

"Mama . . . Mama . . ." Mohamed shook Madame Chief's arm to rouse her, and he checked to see that she was breathing.

Mama opened her eyes, rolled over, and sat up slowly. Alice was asleep on a mat on the floor, her arm slung across the pink doll.

"Is it time to get up already?"

"Yes, Mama. I think it is going to be very hot today, and the doctor said that you should walk now."

Mohamed had found another doctor for Madame Chief and coerced him into coming to the camp to check on her health and give her more medicine. The doctor had stayed overnight, bandaging up several rebels who had engaged ECOMOG soldiers the day before.

"I have already prepared washing water for you," Mohamed said, pointing to a small tub of water on the floor at the foot of the bed.

Madame Chief peered over the edge of the bed at the sleeping child. "Wake up Alice."

Mohamed walked over to Alice and gave her a little push. The girl's eyes flew open, and she scrambled to her feet holding the doll. Her wide-eyed fear immediately turned to a scowl of resentment when she realized that it was Mohamed, not Aaron, who had frightened her.

"No one is going to hurt you, girl," Mohamed huffed and walked to the door.

"Be kind," Madame Chief reminded him as he opened it and left.

Madame Chief walked through the house and noted how quiet it was. There were about one hundred rebels at the camp. The night before they had stayed up late, drinking and sniffing drugs, pumping each other up with stories about how they were going to take back Liberia from Charles Taylor, and trying not to notice how many of them had died that day.

Mohamed stepped off the porch and held Madame Chief's hand as she came down the stairs, shadowed by Alice.

"Where is Joe?"

"He is still sleeping. I will get him," Mohamed replied, turning.

"No, let him sleep," said Madame Chief.

"Did Blaze use the drugs last night?"

"Only a little, Mama."

They walked farther than usual, all the way to the end of the path.

"Let's sit and rest for a while before going back to the house," Madame Chief said.

She sat down on a tree stump. Alice sat down next to her on the bare earth. Mohamed went to a tree, squatted on the ground, and leaned his back against it. He picked up small stones and listlessly threw them at the bushes.

Of the three rebels, Madame Chief had grown to depend on Mohamed the most. He had been appointed to take care of her and had done his job well. She was proud that he had continued to resist coercion to use the drugs and grateful that he had not had to use his gun often. But it bothered her that she had failed to turn him around. She had been successful with other rebels, new recruits like Mohamed, who had deserted the LRFD.

I must try again.

"There is nothing good waiting for you in Monrovia. You know this, Mohamed. You should be with your family in your village, where you are needed."

Mohamed frowned.

"Listen to me."

"Mama, I always listen to you."

They were quiet for a moment.

"There is nothing there either, Mama," Mohamed said finally.

"There are people waiting for you to come home, people who love you. Didn't your uncle promise to teach you how to make shoes?"

"Pipe dreams, Mama. Two of the new recruits told me that no one is living in my village now."

Mohamed picked up another stone and threw it hard. His face twisted with anger and pain.

"I see," said Madame Chief. "So there is nothing I can say to change your mind?" Mohamed stood up. His bottom lip quivered, tears welled up in his eyes.

"Mama, where am I to go? Where? Where, Mama? There is no place for me to go." His voice broke.

Madame Chief reached for him. He turned away.

She began humming a peaceful tribal song. Gradually, Mohamed calmed down. He shoved his hands into his pockets and leaned back against the tree, staring in space. "Forgive me, Mama," he said. "I should not have taken out my frustration on you."

"There is nothing to forgive, Mohamed."

A minute passed. A large golden butterfly with delicate black markings flapped around Mohamed's head.

Mohamed sighed. "They told me that my family ran to their village. My village was burned to the ground. They made some of my relatives dig their own graves before they shot them. I have to stay now and get revenge, Mama. I'm glad that my family got away, but it is not enough. Everything is gone now. The new recruits told me the name of this band of rebels. I have never heard of them. I don't know who is fighting who and for what anymore. Everyone is fighting everyone, and now I am fighting them. I now have a clear reason for fighting."

"How do these boys know this?"

"I overheard them talking about my village, so I asked them."

"What else did they say?"

"My brother told one of them that they were going to Guinea because we have family there. I am hoping there is room for them. My uncle has taken in many already."

The pain in Mohamed's eyes pierced Madame Chief's heart. *He is slipping away from me. The war is taking him.*

"Then you should go to where they are," said Madame Chief, standing. "I am ready to go back now."

Suddenly Joe appeared on the path ahead of them, carrying a stick and mumbling to himself as he thrashed through the bushes.

"Why did you go without me?" he asked Mohamed angrily.

"You were sleeping, man."

Joe brushed past Mohamed roughly.

"Mama, you could have told him to wake me up," he complained.

"Good morning, Joe," Madame Chief said pleasantly.

"Mama, how could you go walking about this place without me?"

"Oh, Joe. It is not such a big deal," Madame Chief said, attempting to humor him.

Joe pointed an accusing finger at Mohamed. "But, Mama, this boy knew it was not right. I should walk with you every day. Someday there will be no more opportunities to do this."

"There will be others," Madame Chief said, walking ahead of him. "I have decided that you and Mohamed will ride with me to my country."

Joe's face brightened. He clapped his hands and strutted, lifting his long legs high at the knee like a dancer on stilts.

They started back to the camp.

*   *   *

8:00 a.m.

Col. Olatungi stopped the convoy at the bottom of a hill. The road leading to the rebels' headquarters was on the other side. Two soldiers jumped out of the jeep and started running toward the summit. After several minutes had gone by, he got out of the jeep and came back to the car Catherine was in. The colonel tapped on the window with his gold ring. The soldier rolled it down. "Get out," Col. Olatungi said to the driver. "I would like to talk to you in private."

"Wait here until I send for her . . ." Catherine overheard the colonel say as they walked away from the car.

After fifteen minutes, the scouting party came back and went directly to the colonel. Catherine's driver lit a cigarette. Catherine glanced at him and noticed envy in his eyes as he watched the other soldiers quickly heading up the road. She peered through her binoculars and watched her army reach the apex of the hill, then disappear over the other side.

"How far away is the camp?"

"Just over the hill."

*   *   *

8:15 a.m.

When the shooting started, Mohamed whirled around and shouted at Joe.

"What's going on?"

"I don't know," Joe replied, looking nervously in the direction of the camp.

Fearing for Mama, they ran back to her. Alice moved close to Madame Chief and took her hand. The gunfire grew in intensity.

"Mama, stay here while Joe and I go see what is happening."

"No. We must stay together," Madame Chief insisted.

"Where is your gun, man?" Joe yelled at Mohamed.

"I left it with Blaze."

"You left it?"

"Well, where's the new gun you were issued, Joe? You were the one so concerned with having a gun."

"And you are the one assigned to walk with Mama," Joe shot back.

"Man, this is bad. Neither of us have a gun." Mohamed turned to Madame Chief. "Mama, I must go see what is happening."

"OK, you go. But, Joe, you stay."

"Mama," Joe began agitated, "I have to go too."

"Go, go," Madame Chief said finally. "But stay with Mohamed. Do not go to the house," she called after him.

"Mama, do not let them leave us," Alice whimpered as Joe and Mohamed disappeared. Her large eyes filled with tears.

"Do not be afraid, child," Madame Chief said. She grabbed the girl's hand, pulled her close to her side, and began walking as fast as she was able.

Lord, have mercy on all of us.

*   *   *

8:30 a.m.

Pop! Pop! Pop! The shots were getting closer. Through the binoculars, Catherine saw soldiers appear at the top of the hill, then shoot at a rebel running ahead of them. Her hand searched for Mama's pendant. She held it tightly.

"Lord, please let nothing happen to Mama," she prayed and wished there had been another way.

*   *   *

8:35 a.m.

Madame Chief's free hand began to tremble as she picked up the pace.

Have mercy, Father, she prayed.

Madame Chief's breath became labored as she pushed herself to walk faster than she knew she should. As she approached the clearing where Mohamed and Joe were crouched behind a bush, she saw the house surrounded by sharpshooters. Bullets poured out of their semiautomatic rifles, biting off pieces of window and doorframes and shattering glass. Rebels lay dead on the porch.

Madame Chief's heart hammered in her chest as she scanned the faces of the rebels shooting from the windows for signs of Blaze.

"Mama, please stay back," Mohamed said.

The back door of the house flew open, and five rebels came running out headlong. The soldiers were on their heels, shooting as they ran. Wounded, the rebels crawled toward the bush. The soldiers caught up with them and shot until their bodies were still.

"Have mercy, Father," Madame Chief whispered. She closed her eyes to block out the horrible sight and prayed that the rebels remaining in the house would surrender.

Suddenly Blaze appeared on the roof, crouched behind the parapet.

"Blaze!" Joe gasped. Mohamed's eyes widened with fear. Madame Chief opened her eyes and moved toward the clearing.

Blaze fired down on the soldiers, hitting one and then another. A soldier with a machine gun returned Blaze's fire, catching him in the chest and shoulder and spinning him around. Blaze's wig sailed off and floated to the ground. All at once soldiers appeared on the roof, ran over to him, and riddled his body with bullets.

Madame Chief grabbed the front of her dress as a sharp pain formed in the center of her chest. "Mama, Mama," Alice cried. Joe and Mohamed rushed toward Madame Chief and caught her under the arms as she staggered. They helped her get to a boulder nearby.

"Get the palm over there," Mohamed shouted at Alice, pointing at a branch lying on the ground. Alice ran to it. She picked it up and scampered back to Madame Chief. "Mama, Mama, please, Mama," she whispered, rapidly fanning. "I am OK," Madame Chief said as her pain began to subside. Madame Chief took a handkerchief from her pocket and wiped away Alice's tears. She put her arms around her shoulders and comforted her. Alice buried her face in Madame Chief's bosom and sobbed. Joe and Mohamed watched silently, dazed and helpless. Madame Chief's eyes traveled to where Blaze's wig lay in the dust. Soldiers approaching the house trampled it.

The remaining rebels came out with their hands in the air. "We will go now," Madame Chief said. Alice reluctantly stepped to the side as Mohamed and Joe helped her up. More gunshots pierced the air. Alice covered her ears, screaming, "No, no!" She ran over to where her doll lay on the ground, picked it up, and backed away.

"We must go," Madame Chief said calmly. "I want to talk to these men."

"No, Mama. They will kill us!" the girl insisted. She ran to Madame Chief, fell to her knees, and grabbed her around the legs, trembling and crying again. Madame Chief placed a hand on Alice's head.

Suddenly soldiers appeared, their guns trained on Mohamed and Joe.

"Hands behind your head. Down on your knees," one ordered. Mohamed and Joe dropped to the ground and stared into the barrels of three guns.

"Madame, are you all right?"

"Yes," she responded.

"Please come with us," one soldier said. "We have been looking for you."

*   *   *

9:15 a.m.

Silence.

Catherine's heart pounded in her chest.

This waiting is killing me. Why are we just sitting here?

"Do you think it's over?" Catherine asked the driver. Annoyed, he turned his head away and looked out the window.

Catherine picked up the binoculars. There was no sign of movement. She opened the door.

"Where are you going?"

"I just want to stretch my legs."

Catherine started up the hill. As she had anticipated, the driver started the car and pulled up beside her.

"Get in."

"I'm not going anywhere. I just want to get closer."

"Get in, woman!"

Catherine glared at him and kept walking.

"Get in. I will drive to the top so that you can take a look."

Catherine obeyed. The car moved slowly up the hill. Through the binoculars, Catherine spotted a rebel on his stomach in the grass. He was aiming at someone in the bush. She turned in the direction of the gun barrel and saw soldiers, a young girl, and Madame Chief.

Mama!

The rebel fired.

"Mama!" Catherine screamed. "Stop the car." She jumped out and ran toward Mama.

The soldiers crouched and returned the fire.

Oh, Lord, not Mama. Please.

Her heart hammered in her chest, and she froze when she saw the soldiers bent over Madame Chief.

Oh, Lord, no.

Alice had fallen on top of Madame Chief when the bullet struck her. Catherine watched as the soldiers gently pulled her lifeless body away from Mama. Numbness began to spread from Catherine's chest to her brain. Mama did not move. A soldier leaned over Mama and attempted to help her up. She pushed them away, sat up, and reached for Alice. The soldiers placed her in Madame Chief's arms. Mama stroked her face, closed the girl's eyes, and prayed.

Catherine ran to Mama and kneeled beside her. Madame Chief held out her hand. Relieved, Catherine wrapped her arms around her, crying.

Madame Chief kissed her forehead.

"It is good to see you, my daughter."

CHAPTER TWENTY-ONE

April 20, 10:00 a.m.
Monrovia

Marcus hung up the phone. It was the last call he needed to make before catching a plane to Liberia. There was sweat on his brow. He carelessly threw his clothes inside his overnight suitcase and closed it. The report from the CIA officer, delineating the details of Madame Chief's rescue, including the measures that had been taken to ensure Catherine's safety, lay on the bed. He picked it up and stuffed it into his jacket pocket as he left his room at Le Méridian.

*   *   *

Marcus's eyes clouded the moment he saw Catherine two hours later in her room at the Mamba Point Hotel.

"Daddy," she said.

He hugged her tightly. Her body felt fragile and small. Finally, Marcus released her. He took a good look at her. Catherine looked tired and worn.

Catherine studied Marcus's face. Unshaven, Marcus looked as if he had not slept in days; the white of his eyes had dulled, his skin had lost its luster. She realized the strain she had placed on him.

I did this to him. I did this to my dad.

Suddenly Catherine felt overwhelmed with sadness. Prior to rushing off to Liberia, she had not thought what she was about to put Marcus through.

"You didn't have to come," Catherine said, not knowing what else to say.

"Yes, I did."

"I'm all right." It was a feeble attempt to reassure him.

"I had to see for myself."

Catherine hugged Marcus again. He blinked back tears. "I'm sorry, Daddy," she said, fighting back her own tears. Her bottom lip trembled, and her chest filled with emotion.

Marcus remembered that Catherine used to hug him this tightly when she was a child. It had been a long time.

"It's OK," he said and managed to smile. He smoothed the hair from her face lovingly then took a seat at a table facing her.

"Would you like some water?" Catherine asked.

"Yes, please."

Catherine opened the bottle for him.

"How's Madame Chief doing?"

"Mama had a mild heart attack," Catherine replied softly.

"It was bound to happen. It could have been worse."

"I didn't think about that part. It didn't register the way it should have after Jules told me. She could have died from the stress, Daddy."

"She'll be OK."

Suddenly Catherine felt very tired.

"I suppose you're going to go back to Mokebe with Madame Chief?" Marcus asked.

"Yes."

"How long are you planning to stay?"

"Not long, just until Mama and I have a chance to talk. Her people have come for her. They're taking her back to Sierra Leone tomorrow. Mohamed and Joe, two of the rebels who took care of her, are riding with her."

"Claypool is letting them go?"

"Not exactly. Soldiers will bring them back to Monrovia after we reach the border, but Mama has talked to him."

Catherine sat down in a chair, opened a bottle of water, and drank part of it.

"Daddy, could you ask one of the embassy secretaries to contact Jeremy, let him know what happened, and have him call Justine? I'd like her to know I'm all right. It's been days since the last time I talked to her, and I can't get an overseas line to hold." In the back of her mind, Catherine knew Justine would tell Clifton the whole story.

The phone rang. Catherine excused herself and took the call.

As Marcus waited, his mind wondered back to the danger Catherine had been in. Even though she was within eyesight, he could not shake the anxiety and helplessness that had taken hold of him the moment he had learned what she had done.

Catherine glanced over at him and smiled.

She's all right, he reassured himself and let go of the feeling. She had not been physically harmed, and as far as he could tell, there were no emotional scars. Still, he felt protective toward her. He finally understood the depth of her relationship with Madame Chief, one so deep she'd risked her life to rescue her. He vowed that from now on, all situations involving Madame Chief would go to the top of his list of priorities, right under matters concerning Catherine.

He also decided to keep a vigilant eye on Sierra Leone. The rebel gang called the Revolutionary United Front, or RUF, had taken firm control of the eastern region of the country. Their brutality and methods of mind control of child soldiers were rumored to surpass that of the warlords of Liberia, and their ranks were growing as they emptied the diamond mines.

"How long are you staying in Liberia?" Catherine asked, hoping Marcus would stay the night.

"Until tomorrow."

"And after that?"

"I haven't gotten that far."

"Daddy, can you ride along with me to Mokebe?"

"Of course."

CHAPTER TWENTY-TWO

April 25
Mokebe, Mama's Village

Nadia, Madame Chief's personal maid, came to Catherine's room early in the morning and told her that Mama wanted to see her. Catherine got dressed and went to Madame Chief's bedroom. Madame Chief was standing on the veranda, looking out at the ocean.

"Yes, Mama?"

"Let's go for a walk," said Madame Chief.

They headed toward the beach, past village folk doing their daily chores and children playing tag amidst a covey of chickens, which scampered away from their little feet.

The blue ocean glistened under the sun. Cloudless skies stretched along the horizon. The white sandy beach, which extended far beyond what the eye could see, gave gently under the soles of Catherine's and Mama's bare feet.

They walked for a while in silence, listening to the waves lapping the shore and breathing the sweet seaweed-infused air. Seagulls circled overhead, their cries echoing in the atmosphere.

"Daughter," Madame Chief said, taking Catherine's hand, "I am glad you are staying until the celebration is over."

"I am too. How are you feeling, Mama?" Catherine said.

"Fair."

They walked farther down the beach, again falling deep in thought.

Catherine thought about how strange life was. Mama had taken care of her, and in a twist of fate, she had taken care of Mama.

She looked at Madame Chief's strong profile as if she was seeing her for the first time after years of separation, knowing that nothing would ever change between them, that even after death they remained connected. But, the guilt she had come to feel about her impulsiveness and the lives that had been lost did not dissipate.

"I feel so sorry for the girl, Alice," Catherine said. acknowledging Mama's grief.

"She was a good girl," Madame Chief said. "Do not blame yourself."

"But she would be alive today if I had not decided to take matters into my hands."

"Perhaps, but we all knew how this would end. Lives would be lost. It is the war, not you, that caused her death. As long as Liberia is consumed by the war, more people who should have a long life will die. It has been this way since the day you left."

"I will have to work it out, Mama."

They walked for a while, listening to the waves.

"Tell me about the anniversary," Madame Chief said finally. "I assume you were here, in Sierra Leone."

"No, I had a layover in Amsterdam. I was there when the anniversary came."

Madame Chief's eyebrows furrowed.

"I was fine," Catherine responded. "A friend was with me."

"I am glad to hear that you were not alone. What did you do for yourself?"

"Nothing special."

"Is that so?" Madame Chief asked, surprised.

"There has been a change in me, Mama. I had an epiphany."

Mama looked perplexed.

"It's hard to explain," Catherine continued. "I was sitting on the couch, thinking about the anniversary and how you had been with me every year from the very beginning. As I began to think about each one, in my mind's eye, I saw you sitting on the tree stump, singing. Suddenly your spirit reached out to mine. It explained something I had not been able to articulate. That epiphany fueled my obsession with finding you. But I don't think I would have behaved so irrationally if rebels had not been involved. It felt like it was happening all over again. You were taken away from me and from your people the same way my friends were taken from me and their families by soldiers. I couldn't believe it. I knew the situation was altogether different, and I waited it out as long as I could. But I couldn't trust anyone to take care of it, not even my father."

"You must tell him what is on your heart. He is not perfect, but he has watched over you in ways that you will never know."

"I know that, Mama. I could have ruined his career. I feel so bad about that."

"Perhaps you had to go through this to see what you have to work out with your father and yourself."

"That's another thing. I've felt my faith returning for some time now, but I was still confused. I thought your rescue was the reason I was coming here, but then I realized that there was another reason. I had come back to Africa on the anniversary to go to Liberia."

Madame Chief nodded. "God and the ancestors were with you. It was time for your wound to heal completely. It was time for the mourning to end. We are guided by His hand. It had to be finished in Liberia, where it began."

"Do you think I should have gone back to Liberia before now?"

"We are God's children. He picks the time and circumstance of our delivery."

"What about my friends? How will I honor them now that I don't need the ritual?"

"You will figure that out on your own," said Mama. "Go back to America and wait. Allow the answer to come to you. It will lead you to something greater."

"Something greater?"

"Yes. Something greater."

*   *   *

All who could come, from every village in Mama's chiefdom, were gathered for the celebration. Madame Chief sat in a chair on a platform that had been constructed for the occasion. The elders and chiefs sat under an open tent. Catherine and Marcus sat with Mama's other guests, conversing with one another. Jules and Celeste arrived as chimes were rung, signaling the beginning of the homecoming festivity.

"I'm so glad you and Jules made it to the celebration," Catherine said to Celeste as they hugged.

"I wouldn't have missed it."

Like thunder the sound of the drums burst into the air. The dense crowd turned and parted. Drummers, playing drums held fast to the front of their bodies by ropes slung over their shoulders, moved in single file toward the platform. Following them, dancers dressed in colorful tie-dyed skirts, matching head wraps, beaded necklaces, and ankle bracelets danced and clapped their hands. Excited, the villagers cheered and applauded as the procession made its way to the platform where Madame Chief sat smiling. When all the performers stood facing Madame Chief, the drumming rose in intensity, then stopped.

"Mama, we honor you!" the lead drummer proclaimed in a booming voice. Everyone who was not already standing stood up and turned toward Madame Chief. In homage, they bowed from the waist. A young chief moved to the center of the gathering and led a call-and-response chant honoring the greatness of the people of Sierra Leone. Afterward singers assembled themselves in front of the crowd and led a song of thanksgiving.

Next the elders spoke, giving honor to the ancestors, praising the men in the village who had valiantly attempted to cross the border to rescue Mama, acknowledging Marcus, and thanking Catherine. The food was blessed, and people moved to the tents where fish stew, chicken, rice, plantain, and cassava leaves were cooking in many large pots.

Marcus and Jules excused themselves and went to stand under a tree to talk in private.

Servers soon came with plates of food. While they ate, Catherine and Celeste made small talk with Madame Chief's other guests. "Let's go for a walk. I need to stretch my legs," Celeste said after they had finished eating and the servers had returned for their empty plates.

"I want to thank you again for introducing me to Bobby," Catherine said when they had cleared the crowd. "I really leaned on him."

"I knew I could count on him. By the way, what did you say to Col. Olatungi to get him to let you go on the rescue?"

"I don't think I said anything in particular," Catherine replied. "Before I left Liberia, Claypool told me that Col. Olatungi knew that the deal the UN had made for Mama's release had gone sour when he agreed to work for me. Everyone was waiting for Charles Taylor to come up with an alternative plan for Mama's rescue, and no one really trusted his judgment. Then I showed up."

"So that's what happened," Celeste said, nodding thoughtfully. "You're a legend among Madame Chief's people now," she added. "The next thing you know, there'll be stories told to little children about you."

Catherine grinned.

"Did you hear about Ester?" Celeste asked.

"I heard that she betrayed Mama."

"The villagers have ostracized her. If they happen to run into her, they act as if they don't know her."

"Mama feels sorry for her," Catherine said. "Ester is just a simple woman. I don't think she knew how far Fofana would go to get his hands on the diamonds."

"It's a shame," said Celeste, shaking her head. "That's probably why she was acting so strangely when she saw you at the Bintumani. She couldn't have felt right about keeping that from Mama."

"Who knows what really happened," Catherine replied, thinking about how ashamed Ester had looked.

"What happened to the rebels who took Mama?" Celeste asked Catherine as they sat down.

"One of them died during the fighting, the other two are being held in custody. Mama made Claypool promise to do what he could for them. The leader disappeared after he got ransom for kidnapping the UN representative and his staff."

A girl about ten years old came over. She stopped and stood looking up at Catherine. Her beautiful large eyes were wide with admiration.

"Hello, little sister," Catherine said.

"Did you really fight the rebels?" the girl blurted out.

"I went with the soldiers when they went to get Mama," Catherine responded.

"But they say you saved Mama," the girl insisted.

Catherine sighed.

"It's a long story. I . . ."

Instantly Catherine felt a jab from Celeste's elbow. Catherine glanced at her out of the corner of her eye. The expression on Celeste's face was unmistakable, *Just go with it.*

"Yes," Catherine replied, "I saved Mama."

The girl beamed and smiled broadly. "Can I give you a hug?"

Catherine bent down as the girl wrapped her arms around her waist and hugged her fiercely. Satisfied, the youngster smiled and walked away.

"Let's go back," Celeste suggested.

Everyone had just about finished eating. Flatbeds holding large electric generators were being rolled into position next to huge speakers, and the musicians began setting up.

*   *   *

Marcus and Jules watched the band set up for a moment.

"How's Catherine doing?" Jules asked.

"She's in good spirits."

Jules took a deep breath and exhaled slowly. "Thank God it's over, Marcus. I should have had more respect for her feelings about Madame Chief."

"Don't beat up yourself too much. We've both learned a few lessons," Marcus replied, glancing in the direction of his daughter.

"I spoke with Claypool. He said Catherine came up short when she settled the account with Col. Olatungi but, it was taken care of by an anonymous donor."

Marcus frowned.

"Don't worry Marcus. Our people are on it already. We can't afford to leave this hanging. We'll find out who and why. Claypool said Catherine's not comfortable with it either. She probably won't rest until she knows who helped her."

"Keep me posted."

An elder approached Marcus.

"I would like to introduce myself to you. My name is Issac Jawara. I want to personally thank you for everything you have done for Mama over the years. My daughter is the one who writes to you about Mama's needs. She is her secretary."

The two men shook hands. "I will continue to be a friend to Madame Chief," Marcus assured him.

"Please come to my home before you leave Mokebe. We are making special gifts for you and your daughter. They will be ready tomorrow."

The elder turned and walked away, his robes flowing around him.

"Testing . . . testing . . . ," a guitarist spoke into a microphone.

"It looks like the band is ready to play," said Jules.

"Hello, everybody. How's de body?"

The crowd cheered.

"OK now. Let's get right to it. Ah one . . . ah two . . ."

The band launched into a popular song with an African Caribbean beat. Young people jumped up first; then villagers of all ages moved onto the dance area. Jules took Celeste's hand and led her into the crowd. Catherine danced in her seat, moving to the beat and clapping her hands. Happy, she closed her eyes and let the music move her body.

"May I have this dance?"

Catherine opened her eyes.

"Oh my god!" she exclaimed in disbelief, unable to take her eyes off Clifton's face. He grinned and extended his hand.

Laughing, Catherine slid off the chair and melted into Clifton's outstretched arms. Breathing him in, she whispered, "What are you doing here?"

"First I got tired of waiting for you to come back," he replied, giving her a squeeze. "And then . . ."

"Then what?"

"I got scared that with all your crusading, you might not come back. So I decided to just show up and let you know."

"Let me know what?"

"That I'm in need of a little rescuing myself."

Catherine smiled.

That can be arranged, she thought as Clifton leaned forward to kiss her. As their lips met, Catherine caught a glimpse of Mama.

She was smiling too.

POSTSCRIPT

In April 1992, the RUF—backed by Charles Taylor, Liberia's president—waged war against Sierra Leone's established government. Fourteen years later, in March of 2006, Taylor was jailed for war crimes against Sierra Leone for his role in backing that ruthless rebel movement. That same year—twenty-two years after the first coup d'état in Liberia—Ellen Johnson-Sirleaf was elected president of Liberia, and that country moved forward in an effort to recover socially and economically.

Catherine testified before Liberia's Truth and Reconciliation Commission, which was formed to aid the people of Liberia in finding ways to reconcile years of human rights violations.

ABOUT THE AUTHOR

Clara Whaley Perkins is a practicing psychologist and author. She earned her Ph.D. at Temple University. With her husband and son, she has traveled the cities and bush of many African countries. She lives in Philadelphia, Pennsylvania, where she is working on her second novel.

CPSIA information can be obtained at www.ICGtesting.com
Printed in the USA
BVOW030110290911

272404BV00001B/2/P